WELCOME TO THE SPLATTER CLUB

EDITED BY:

K. TRAP JONES

ISBN: 978-1-940250-43-4

Artwork by K. Trap Jones
    www.theevilcookie.com

Interior Layout by Lori Michelle
    www.theauthorsalley.com

Printed in the United States of America

First Edition

Visit us on the web at:
www.bloodboundbooks.net

ALSO FROM
K. TRAP JONES:

The Sinner

The Harvester

The Big Bad

The Drunken Exorcist

TABLE OF CONTENTS

SPLATTER PARTY

JOHN MCNEE

NADIA WAS THE one who answered the door the first time. She had gone to the bathroom to escape Kyle and the others. She knew it wouldn't be long before someone came looking for her, maybe only a few minutes, but at least that would be some respite.

She was dizzy from the alcohol and stumbled a little as she sat down on the edge of the bathtub, nearly falling in. A bottle of beer was in her hand and she stared at it sadly while trying to decide whether to put it to her lips. She'd been drinking all night and this was as far as it had gotten her—drunk enough to fall down, but not drunk enough to enjoy herself.

Nadia set the bottle on the floor and took her phone out of her pocket. From the wall behind her, came the pounding electronic bass of a new song. Her phone told her it was 3:05am, but the crowd in the next room sounded like they were only just getting started. She scrolled through her contacts, looking for someone who could come save her from the tedium, but she knew in her heart it was pointless. It was too late—or too early—and they were much too far from town. She could either call herself a taxi she couldn't afford or wait until Stacy and Declan decided they'd had enough and hitch a ride with them.

But how long might that take? Two hours? Three? Four? *Maybe*, she thought, *I'll get lucky and they'll burn themselves out in one.*

A massive cheer from the lounge suggested this was unlikely to be the case.

Rising to her feet—back up onto the stupid high heels she was resolutely still wearing—she crossed to the sink and took a long look at the girl in the mirror. Little red dress and black leather jacket, big blonde hair already looking like it had lost a third of its volume, and smeared make-up. She'd laid it on thick, intentionally. At the start of the night it had looked striking. Now it looked like it was pulling her down, weighing so heavy on her eyes and lips they might slide right off her face into the sink. Topping the whole image off was the setting—a cramped, stained and dimly-lit bathroom in a council flat, painted the color of regurgitated spinach. The ideal place, she thought, to find a wilted flower like her.

"Well," she told herself, "You wanted a party."

This was true. After the week, month, *year* she'd had, she was desperate for a party. A real party with cheap drink and big laughs and dancing and drugs and maybe a little sex, who knew? But Saturday came and nothing was happening. Friends weren't keen. Suitable venues were unavailable. She'd accepted an invitation from Stacy and Declan to hit the town with them, in the hopes it might lead somewhere. But it had led here.

A fist hammered at the door. "Nadia! You all right in there?" Stacy's voice.

"I'm fine," she replied. "Give me a minute!"

"Okay, but hurry up. Shug needs a piss!" Stacy laughed and Nadia heard Shug yelling at her to shut up from the kitchen.

Ah yes, Shug. The one who liked her. The nice one. Nicer than the other one, in any case.

She had been introduced to him at the club Stacy and Declan had taken her to—a half-empty dive whose DJ couldn't even feign enthusiasm. Shug was a friend of a friend, there with other friends who promised a real party was just getting started across town.

It was already late, but Nadia let him get her hopes up that a great night could still be had. They went in two taxis—her with Stacy, Declan and Shug in one, his friends in the other. All Shug asked—and no-one minded—was that they make a quick stop at his flat on the way, where his drug-dealing flatmate could provide all they needed to ensure the party went with a bang.

A quarter of an hour later they were standing in Shug's living room, being introduced to Kyle, who sat—shirtless and skinny—in a leather sofa on the other side of a coffee table littered with pills and powders in plastic bags.

"There's beers in the fridge," he said, speaking to everyone but staring directly at Nadia. "You'll stay for one drink, won't you?"

One drink became two—it wasn't smart to reject the hospitality of drug dealers after all— and Nadia had already realized they wouldn't be going anywhere else long before Shug got the text to say the party had been canceled.

"No worries," Kyle said, as he cranked up the volume on his sound system. "We can have our own party right here, eh?"

Now Nadia shook her head at the reflection in the bathroom mirror. "Oh, you silly girl," she said. "You know nothing good ever happens after 3am."

Turning away from the sad sight, she bent down to collect the beer. It was still full, still cold. She knew she had a decision to make as to how best to navigate the coming hours. She could sober up and wait it out, playing nice but keeping her guard up. Or she could commit to the madness and the danger and hope that in the midst of whatever was to come, she found some measure of enjoyment. There was a certain satisfaction to be found, she knew, in willingly making bad decisions.

She was still in two minds on the matter as she put the bottle to her lips, tilted her head back and drained it.

She walked out of the bathroom to the opening strains of a new song and Stacy's cry of "I fucking love this", which was very nearly enough to persuade her to turn around again. She didn't, but then, while she was still in the hall, making her way back to the living room, there was a knock at the front door, surely too quiet for any of the others to hear.

She opened it and was met by a small, middle-aged man, clasping his hands, as though in prayer. "Please," he said. It was the only thing he said for several seconds as he stood staring at her, a pained smile on his face, emphatically shaking his hands. He had gray hair and a long, tanned face, and was wearing a knitted jumper beneath a brown polyester suit that might have been older than he was. "Please!" His lips trembled as he strained for another word. It was clear English wasn't his first language, but his next sentence confirmed it. "*Da muzica*," he said. "*Da muzica mai incet te rog!*"

Nadia said nothing.

Sighing, then cursing in his native tongue, the man pointed at the floor and tried again. "I . . . down!"

"You okay, Nadia?" Stacy asked, coming to her side, regarding the man like an overzealous beggar who'd accosted them in the street.

"*Muzica*!" The man was pointing to the living room now, in the direction of the music. "Too big. Please. My mother..!"

"Who is it?" Shug called.

"I think it's your neighbor," Stacy answered and pulled Nadia away, leading her into the living room.

Shug passed them on the way and Nadia did her best not to listen in. Easy enough, with the music cranked up so high. Stacy joined Declan on the couch opposite Kyle, while she perched on the arm. There was room to sit beside Kyle, but she wasn't about to take advantage of that.

"What's going on?" he asked, not looking up from the joint he was rolling. He'd put a shirt on since she and the others had arrived, but that was the only concession he'd made to civility.

"Your neighbor's complaining about the noise," Steph said.

Kyle scoffed. "Fuck that prick. Some nerve coming up here and telling me what to do. Cunt only moved in this week and thinks he can shout the odds."

"Maybe it's a bit loud?" Declan suggested.

"Is it fuck!" Kyle leaned down to the speaker at his side to turn it up higher. "*Now* it's too loud!"

He laughed and so did Declan and Stacy. Nadia wanted to—she wanted to join in, give in to the mood—but could only manage a smile. She was thinking of the man at the door.

She heard it slam and then Shug reappeared. "I told him to fuck off," he said. "I think he understood, but he wasn't happy about it."

"Polish prick." Kyle sneered.

He's not Polish, Nadia wanted to say, because she knew. But she said nothing.

"You want another beer, Nadia?" Shug asked.

She didn't, but smiled at him and nodded.

"Fucking wanker comes over here and thinks he can boss me around, tell me what to do," Kyle continued, flicking his lighter on as he put the joint between his lips. "But if he doesn't like it here, living in *my* fucking country, he can just leave! That's the difference between me and him. Cunt doesn't know how lucky he is."

Nadia frowned. "Why can't you leave?" She had to shout to make herself heard.

Kyle gave her a look like he'd forgotten she was there and was delighted all over again to see her, his eyes roving over her from head to toe. Then he reached down to his ankle and pulled up the leg of his tracksuit bottoms to reveal the electronic tag. "Can't go more than 200 meters away during the day. And I can't leave the house after dark."

Nadia nodded. "Because of drugs?"

He smiled. "A few different things." He lit the joint and took a long drag, then held it out to her.

She hesitated, only because she felt the eyes of her friends on her. As if they'd never seen her smoke a joint before.

Ignoring their concern, she stood and crossed the room to take it. And as her fingers brushed against Kyle's, he shuffled, rather theatrically, over to one side of the sofa—a gesture that could only be read as strong encouragement for her to sit down beside him.

It wasn't the drugs Stacy and Declan had been worried about, she realized now, too late. She knew they both liked Shug, who at this moment was still fetching beers. They liked him so much that they would have been delighted if she was to hook up with him. But they were *scared* of Kyle. And she had just walked into his trap.

Knowing she couldn't well take the joint—which he had left dangling between her fingers—and go back across to the other side of the room, she sank down into the spot beside him, maintaining as much distance as she could, which wasn't much. She did her best to look at ease while he gave her a close-quarters inspection, gaze lingering on her thighs.

"So what's your story?" he asked. It wasn't hard to see what the others found so frightening about him. Everything about him looked sharp and mean. His smile, when he showed it to her, looked meanest of all.

Before she could say anything, there was another knock at the door. Much louder this time, more insistent, perhaps more desperate. At least that's how it sounded to her.

"Aw for fuck sake!" Kyle said. "Has this prick got a fucking death wish or what?"

No-one else in the room was up for voicing an opinion on the subject.

The sound came again—two fists hammering rapid-fire against the door.

"Fuck this," Kyle said. Then he was up on his feet, out of the room and striding down the hall.

"Uuuhh?" said Declan, on behalf of everyone left behind.

Nadia heard Shug call from the kitchen, then the sound of the door being thrown open. She turned the volume down on the speaker and maneuvered herself into a position where she could see what was happening out in the hallway.

She could see Kyle at the doorway and the hands of his neighbor, shaking, fingers splayed, as he yelled, "My mother sleeps! *Da muzica! Da muzica mai incet te rog*! Please! My mother! *Stapanul meu trebuie sa doarma!*"

"Fuck your mother," said Kyle. Then he grabbed the man by the collar and head-butted him in the face. The attack was delivered with such force that, despite the roar of the music behind her, Nadia could hear the crunch as his forehead connected with the man's nose. She heard his awful cry as he collapsed to his knees.

"Oh my God," she said, putting a hand to her mouth.

"What's happening?" Stacy asked. Neither she nor Declan could see from where they were sitting.

"He hit him. I think he broke his nose."

"Fuck off," said Declan, grinning in disbelief.

The front door slammed and Kyle re-entered the living room, wiping at his forehead then checking his fingers for blood. "Cunt."

"What did I miss?" asked Shug, appearing behind him.

"Kyle just kicked the shit out of your neighbor," said Stacy, reaching over and snatching a beer from his hand.

"Seriously?"

Kyle shrugged. "A wee warning, that's all."

"He broke his nose," said Nadia, eyes on Kyle.

"See what I break if he comes back," he said. There was no threat in his voice. It was a calm statement of truth. "Who turned the music down?"

Shug and the others were laughing as Kyle bent to the speaker and cranked up the volume. They were at the stage of intoxication and sleep deprivation where everything seemed hilarious.

"You're fucking mental," Shug yelled. "What happens if he calls the police?"

"He gets deported?" Kyle suggested. "He's not going to call the police. Right now, he'll be crying to his mum."

No, Nadia thought. *He won't.* She said nothing, but while the others were arguing, laughing and joking, she was thinking about what the man had said. *Stapanul meu trebuie sa doarma.*

She didn't like to tell people she was Romanian. Her family had relocated when she was eight-years-old and she had worked intensely in the subsequent years to eradicate her accent, assimilating fully into the fashions and culture of the west of Scotland.

People liked to pretend this country didn't have a problem with racism or xenophobia, that it welcomed and accepted immigrants. Nadia had seen enough as a child to know this was bullshit. Bigots were everywhere. Overt and covert. If she could conceal her true ethnicity from them, she would. She didn't need the hassle.

She still slipped up, every now and then, not so badly that anyone noticed. The voice in her head was still Romanian and there were certain English words it seemed she would always have issues with, for as long as she lived. She still sometimes said *own* when she meant *owe*. She still sometimes said *coach* when she meant couch.

Kyle's neighbor clearly had a very limited vocabulary, but still made the same kind of errors, mistaking one word with another that sounded similar.

"My mother sleeps." Those had been his words in English. But when he'd spoken in Romanian, he hadn't said *mother*.

He'd said *master*.

She could have asked him what he meant. The first time he came to the door, when she answered, she could have translated for him. But that would have meant exposing herself. Now she could only wonder at what he'd really intended to say and what it implied.

And what did it imply?

"Here," Shug said.

She blinked and realized he was in front of her, holding out a beer. She snatched it, put it to her mouth and did her best to drown her thoughts in alcohol.

"You okay?" he asked.

"Yes," she said, gasping as she took the bottle from her lips. "But I wish I wasn't."

"What?"

"I hear you!" Kyle clapped, grinning wide. He grabbed some bags of pills from the coffee table. "Who's ready to get fucked up?"

His last word was spoken in the same moment the lights went out. The music stopped. Darkness and silence seized control of the room.

Stacy screamed. Declan laughed. Nadia said nothing. A hand brushed her arm and she grabbed at it. Shug. "It's okay," he said.

"What's happening?" she asked, shouting before realizing she didn't have to. Everything was quiet now.

"I don't believe it," Kyle said. He remained where he was—a jagged silhouette among the shadows. He laughed and Nadia imagined she could see his grin, slicing white and sharp through the darkness. There was no humor in the sound. A laugh of disbelief, twisting to fury. "I don't fucking believe it! That Polish cunt!"

"He did this?" Stacy's voice, though Nadia couldn't see her.

"Of course he fucking did," Kyle snapped back and began marching out of the room, down the hall, finding his way through the gloom as confidently as if he'd been blind all his life.

"How . . . how could he do that?" asked Declan.

Nadia felt Shug move beside her. He squeezed her hand and pulled her up onto her feet as he followed Kyle. "I don't know. There's a fuse box downstairs, by the main door. He could've messed with that?"

The others fell in behind her, taking out their phones to shine some light as they all chased Kyle out of the flat, into the common stairwell. Nadia heard the echo of his steps as he went down the stairs but couldn't see him. He was comfortable moving through the darkness. Like an insect, she thought.

"Kyle," Shug called, shining his phone's torch over the bannister and lighting the scene below a dim blue. If they were right about the neighbor tampering with the fuse box, it would have affected the whole building, but no one from any of the other flats had come out of their doors, alerted by the power cut.

Nadia supposed they were all in their beds, as she wished she was.

"Hey!" The noise of a bony fist pounding against the door to the flat below was amplified by the stone walls and stairs, sounding almost like gunshots. "Open up, ya wee prick!"

With Shug in front and the others behind her, Nadia had little choice but to go with the group down to the landing where Kyle stood, venting his rage against his neighbor's locked door.

"Kyle, come on," said Shug.

"Even if he doesn't phone the police, someone will," said Steph.

When Kyle turned to face them, he was wide-eyed and spitting, froth dripping from his lips. "If he thinks he's safe in there, he's got another fucking thing coming! I will tear the wee shite apart!" Nadia had never in her life seen anyone so angry—a walking, wailing personification of rage. As the rest of them looked on, astonished, he launched his entire body at the door and screamed. "Prick!"

Shug grabbed him as he rebounded, having failed to even rattle the door in its frame. "Fucking calm down! We need to get the power back first. Have you checked the fuse box?"

Kyle wiped his mouth with his hand. "No, I haven't. But I'll bet you it's completely fucked."

He started down the stairs and the others—the rest of the merry caravan—fell in behind him. With Kyle focused on finding the fuse box and Shug focused on Kyle, Nadia did her best to pull back and whisper to Stacy. "We don't need to be here for this."

"I was thinking the same thing," she replied.

Thank God! "Do you want to call a taxi?"

"I would, but I'm not getting any reception in here."

Nadia nodded and took out her own phone to make the call. Then she stopped, staring dumbly at the screen. "Neither am I."

Shug and Kyle were a few steps below them at this point. "Wait," Shug said, a breathy urgency in his voice.

Kyle stopped. "What's that?" he asked.

A wall of darkness was rising to meet them, taking one stair at a time, ascending at the speed of an unhurried pensioner.

"You seeing this?" Kyle said.

No one replied, but no one had to. They all saw it and knew it was something strange and dangerous. They had been in darkness for several minutes now. The light from their phones wasn't so strong that it fully penetrated the shadowy depths of the stairwell.

But whatever rose to meet them now was something more than shadow. Not an emptiness. Not a void. A *presence*. Its black substance teemed with an unquantifiable energy that intrigued as much as it repelled.

Nadia didn't blame Kyle for reaching out his hand toward it. She felt the same impulse herself. The same *need* bubbling in her veins to touch the darkness and feel its gentle caress.

"Stop!" Shug, at least, was not so easily seduced. "Don't!"

Kyle froze at his friend's insistence, still holding out his hand, but no longer advancing. He turned his head to look at the others. "What is it?"

Before anyone could voice a guess, a spear of black sprouted from the advancing wall and glanced upon his finger with a touch as brief and gentle as a kiss.

"*Piele.*"

The voice was male and low. It came not from below, but from all around them, rumbling in the walls and the steps under their feet as the hidden speaker teased out the word. If any of the others knew what it meant, it didn't show in their faces. But Nadia knew.

Skin.

"What the fuck!" Kyle leaped back at the entity's touch, colliding with the others as they too made to retreat.

They raced back up stairs, toward the safety of the top flat, halting only when Kyle gave out a pained shriek. They turned, all training the lights from their phones on him, a few steps below them. His face was twisted in pain. He raised his hand and they all saw the cause.

His index finger had been slashed. A strip of skin two inches long flapped loosely against the wound, which leaked blood over his knuckles and into the palm of his hand. As they watched, the strip pulled taught and then circled his finger, ripping more skin from muscle. It unfurled, like the peeling of an orange, in one spiraling ribbon, exposing the soft, wet flesh beneath. The sound it made was like tearing paper.

Kyle let out a howl of uncomprehending pain—the others supplying an echoing chorus of their own—and grasped his finger with his other hand, squeezing it tight. But then the skin was blown from his arm like leaves on the wind. His scalp peeled back from his skull, his face split apart and now the others were staring into a mask of howling red flesh, bared teeth and wide, unblinking eyes.

Nadia flinched as liquid spattered her face and clothes. It took her a moment to realize it was blood.

"Fuck!" Shug screamed. The closest to Kyle, he spun about and blew past the others, racing up the stairs to return to the flat.

They all followed, leaving Kyle to the embrace of the darkness and the agonizing rebellion of his own skin as it liberated itself from every inch of his body.

The darkness came after them. In the confusion, Nadia had found herself at the back of the group and she could sense the thing, the presence—whatever it was—close behind her, matching her speed, snapping at her heels. If it touched her, she knew she would die. Up ahead, Shug reached the door to the flat and dashed inside, pulling Stacy in behind him. Near the top landing, Declan tripped and half-fell. Nadia sped past him, grateful that he had stumbled, that if anyone was to become a victim, it would be him and not her. As she ran into the flat, she heard the others screaming his name. She turned and saw what they had seen.

The darkness had fashioned another thin finger for itself. It tapped Declan on the top of the head as the same bowel-loosening voice from before announced, "*Oase.*"

Bones.

Declan, his face a vision of pale terror, tried to run, but with the first step he took, they all heard his ankle snap under his weight. He threw his hand up to the wall to catch himself as he fell, but his wrist shattered from the impact, broken shards of bone erupting from his forearm, gleams of white in a blooming mist of red.

He rebounded, hitting the stairs hard on his side, smashing his shoulder, the shock wave coursing up and out across his chest, breaking ribs into splinters. His head bounced off the top step, making a sound like an egg as it was cracked open.

Stacy screamed his name but didn't run to help. None of them did. The instinct for self-preservation was too strong. They could only stand at the door and watch as he lifted his broken head and turned a glazed eye toward them.

His jaw hung low and loose, fractured in a dozen places. When he tried to speak, his tongue pushed out a mouthful of shattered teeth.

If he managed to say anything, they never heard it. Shug threw himself against the door and slammed it shut. Nadia didn't realize she was still screaming until she ran out of breath.

"It's okay." Shug's face was gray, his eyes wide. "We're safe. We're safe." It sounded like a plea more than certainty.

"Declan!" Stacy howled the name through a wretched sob that shook her whole body. For a moment, she looked certain to collapse into hysterics, weeping and pissing on the floor. But with a sharp intake of breath, she blinked and in a measured tone, said, "We have to get out."

Nadia, still in shock, trying to rationalize what she had just seen, didn't have time to take in what had been said or respond to it, before Stacy shoved past her, running into the living room.

"We have to get out," she repeated, racing for the windows. The night beyond was black. No streetlights, no stars. "We need help!"

"No, Stacy," Shug yelled, realizing too late what she was about to do. "Stacy, don't!"

She threw open the window and the black came in to meet her. Its finger glanced upon her cheek. "*Sânge*," it said.

Blood.

The darkness retreated for a moment, hanging back to let the spectacle play out. Stacy, still facing the window, let out a quiet groan of despair, then lifted her hands to her face.

"Stacy?" Nadia hissed. She held her phone out, casting its beam into the room, but she was too afraid to advance.

She watched as her friend turned, slowly, shuffling on unsteady feet, to face the light. Red tears were streaming from her eyes. Blood trickled from her nostrils and the corners of her trembling mouth. She held out her hands to reveal blood-smeared palms.

Nadia felt Shug's hand on her arm. "Come on," he said.

But her attention was still on Stacy, staring as blood flooded her eyes, trickled from her ears, poured from her nose. It spilled down her thighs and pattered on the floor between her legs. With each halting step she took, the flow increased, till it was a gush, soaking her hair and clothes. It oozed from her pores like sweat, painting her skin crimson. When she opened her mouth to scream, there was no air. Only liquid.

"Fucking come on!" Nadia finally moved when Shug forced her, dragging her backward down the hall to the bathroom. The vision of Stacy in scarlet was obscured as darkness swept across the room in pursuit.

Shug threw open the bathroom door and shoved her in ahead of him. She stumbled against the sink and fell onto the edge of the bathtub. Somewhere, at the back of her mind, she dimly registered the fact that it had been less than half an hour since she'd been in this same spot. And how things had changed.

Shug tried to slam the door and it bounced back open, colliding with an empty beer bottle on the floor. He kicked the bottle out of the way and tried again. This time, he succeeded, pulling the door shut a split second after the darkness kissed his hand.

Nadia stood. "It got you."

He shook his head and wiped his hand on his shirt. "No, it didn't. I'm fine. We're going to be . . . "

"*Organele*," the darkness said, purring the word from the other side of the door.

Organs.

Shug shook his head again, casting a spray of sweat from his hair. His expression was insistent. Defiant. "No. No. We're going to be okay."

If Nadia could have retreated from him, she would have. But there was nowhere for her to go. This was it. This repulsive bathroom was where they would both die.

He stepped up to her and grabbed her again around the shoulders. "Listen to me, Nadia," he said. "Listen to me!"

She wondered if he even knew what he was going to say.

"We're going to survive. You hear me?"

From the other side of the door, she thought she could hear laughter.

"We're going t—" Vomit exploded from his mouth. The torrent, an acidic soup of beer, vodka and half-digested pizza, splashed across Nadia's neck and chest.

She screamed, shoved him away, and fell backward into the bathtub. Shug stumbled away in the opposite direction, collapsing against the toilet, still vomiting, throwing up bigger and darker chunks. The slime cascading from his mouth turned red, then black, then reduced to a dribble. It coated every inch of the floor. His bloodshot eyes looked relieved for a moment, then widened in horror. He coughed and gagged and heaved. His throat swelled. He opened his mouth for the second wave, disgorging thick loops of pink and red flesh. His intestines made heavy slaps when they hit the linoleum.

Nadia wanted to look away, but for reasons she couldn't fathom, her eyes remained open. She kept watch until all of Shug's internal organs sat in a pile before him, till he was turned inside out, till he was dead, his head resting on the toilet seat. Then she waited for the darkness to find her.

It didn't take long.

A click sounded from the door and it swung slowly open. She drew herself back into the end of the tub, hugging her knees to her chest, whimpering softly as the darkness eased its way into the room, curling its way between the beams of light from their discarded phones, twisting and turning like sentient smog.

"No," she moaned, choking on her tears. "No, please . . . No . . . " It wasn't fair.

The darkness formed a claw.

"No . . . " She didn't deserve this.

It made a fist.

"Please . . . " All she had wanted . . .

It stretched out a single finger.

"*Voiam doar o petrecere!*" Her outburst was a howl of rage. She screamed it at the top of her lungs, shaking with the volume of her own voice.

All I wanted was a party!

She wept, waiting for the touch of death. Ready to be dealt her excruciating fate.

It didn't happen.

When, after several long seconds of silence, she opened her eyes, she found that the darkness had retreated slightly. Its claw had morphed into a slender hand, ponderously rubbing its thumb and forefinger.

"You're . . . Romanian?" the darkness said, speaking in their shared language.

She could only nod in response.

The darkness sighed. "I wish you had said earlier. It is one thing

14

when a guest in a strange land teaches a lesson to rude and unwelcoming hosts. It is quite another to exact the same punishment on a fellow traveler"

"Please," Nadia whispered, again in her native tongue. "Please let me live."

And, after a moment's thought, the darkness laughed. "Oh, I think we can do better than that."

The darkness asked her to stand and she stood. It told her to strip and she did, peeling off her jacket, red dress and underwear. The darkness turned on the shower and she stepped into the spray, rinsing Kyle's blood from her hair and face, washing Shug's vomit from her neck, shoulders and chest. When she was clean, the darkness handed her a towel and told her to dry herself.

Then it said, "Come downstairs."

She went, guided by the shadows. She stepped over Shug's body to reach the hall, saw the huddled form of Stacy in the gloom and went out into the stairwell. She was careful not to trip over Declan's mangled carcass as she descended and did her best to ignore the sprawled, skinless corpse of Kyle.

The door to the flat below stood open. She entered and met the neighbor, who held a handkerchief to his broken nose. He made a weary appraisal of her naked body and directed her into the next room. It appeared empty but was bathed in ruby light. The polished floor, walls, and ceilings stretched out further than she knew could be possible, given the constraints of the building.

"Come," the darkness said.

She moved forward, further, into the room's ever-expanding red depths. When she looked behind her, she could no longer see the door by which she had entered.

"On your knees."

She lowered herself to the floor.

"So . . . You wanted a party. Is that so?"

Her mouth was dry. She licked her lips before speaking. "Yes."

"Call me Master."

"Yes, Master."

There was a snap from over her shoulder—the sound of a cigarette lighter. She turned and saw Kyle, skinless and dead, standing over her. Declan, a sluggish skin sack of broken bones, stood behind him, arm in arm with Stacy, her still-seeping blood stained the floor behind her like the trail of a slug. And beside her, his organs still hanging in a great, knotted clump from his distended jaw, was Shug.

Kyle was lighting a joint, the same one from earlier. Blood had seeped into the paper, turning it red. Exhaling smoke, he took it from his lips and held it out to her.

She heard her Master say, "Then you shall have one."

Police came in the morning, alerted by residents from other flats who had spotted blood stains on the stairs and gone to investigate. Nobody reported hearing any sounds of argument or violence during the night—at least, nothing beyond the usual disturbances the gentleman on the top floor was known to make.

The flat beneath his was known to have been empty for some time. No one could confirm if anyone was currently living there. On entry, police found a trio of unfurnished rooms with bare floorboards and no curtains. In the largest were four mutilated dead bodies and one nude young woman, completely covered—as was the room itself—in blood.

Later, when examined by a medical team, DNA from each of her friends—including blood, bone, spit, skin and semen—would be found in every one of her orifices.

Responding officers said she was laughing maniacally when they found her and spoke only three words to them before slipping into unconsciousness.

"Best. Party. Ever!"

THE BIG BAD BOY

PATRICK WINTERS

HERE SHE WAS, only a half hour into her Friday night shift, and Maisie already had a gun pointed at her head.

As if that weren't bad enough, she'd just peed herself, and the tears were starting to tingle in her wide eyes as she stood there, rigid and terrified behind the checkout.

"Do what I say, and I promise I won't hurt you!" the ski-masked gunman shouted. But to Maisie, the dire urgency in his voice—and the way the revolver shook in his hand—didn't match up with the promise. She managed to nod, anyway, hoping to Heaven he was telling the truth.

A sudden rumble sounded out in the Dollar Stop and Maisie jumped, shutting her eyes and squealing through gritted teeth, thinking the gunman just broke his promise and had taken a shot at her. But when she realized she was still standing (and breathing), the truth of the noise sunk in. It hadn't been a gunshot; it was a harsh roiling coming from the masked man's big gut.

He certainly wasn't the usual type of crook you'd see, at least not on those late-night cop dramas. They were always gruff-voiced and thin, lithe and able to make quick getaways. This one sounded youthful and nasally, and he was portly—to the extreme. Maisie figured his pants had to be size 42, at least. They looked awfully tight about his wide waist. His pudgy hand engulfed the grip of his gun, his trigger finger stuffed into the frame, and the skin about his eyes and mouth puffed out from under the strained mask.

The gunman's stomach unleashed another growl, as though the Native American on his poor football jersey was trying to speak to them. The man bent over in discomfort as the grumbling drew out, the seams of his dark jacket actually splitting as he cringed in pain. He kept the gun on Maisie, in spite of whatever was wrong with him, and managed to bark at her again.

"Get out from behind there! Now!"

Maisie flinched as he shook the gun in emphasis. Her limbs finally loosened, letting her scurry out and around from the station. The gunman took a few lurching steps her way as she crept forward, his bulk swaying like a pendulum. He kind of reminded her of one of those fertility goddess statues she'd seen in her World Civ course last semester; the comparison could have almost made her laugh, if she wasn't busy soaking her leggings again.

"Please, don't . . . " Maisie began, but she couldn't finish the sentence. "Wh-what do you want?"

She'd been right by the register, but he hadn't demanded she open it. So, if he wasn't after money, then what *was* he after?

"Over to aisle six. Move it!"

Maisie scurried around him as he lowered the gun, holding it at waist-level. He followed her as she headed for the aisle of bread and snack cakes.

She stopped in the mouth of the aisle, dozens of mascots from Little Debbie, Sunbeam, and the like smiling at her misfortune from their packaging.

"The Little Devils," the gunman said. He nodded down toward the center of the aisle, where that particular brand of sweets was arranged on the shelves. Maisie hurried over to them and then turned around to face the gunman. She shrugged at him, lost to her fear and growing confusion.

"Grab them!" he said, jutting his gun out at the snack cakes. "The Big Bad Boys. Hell, all of them!"

Maisie looked at the dozens of Little Devil boxes before her. The cartoon Satan stamped across each of them grinned at her, winking and promising that the product was "Devilishly Delicious!" The Big Bad Boys—newer cakes, triple-layered with crème—had much tubbier devils on the boxes, rubbing their bellies and declaring the cakes to be "Sinfully Scrumptious!"

In that moment, Maisie's surprise trumped her fear, and she turned back to the gunman. "You're robbing us for *junk food*?"

"I don't wanna *eat* them!" the man yelled, making her shrink back. "I wanna *burn* the bastards! Get rid of them! And you're gonna help me. Now, start grabbing!"

The revolver's barrel swung back to her as Maisie reached for the boxes, snatching them up and cradling them in the nook of her arm, squeezing and holding as many against her chest as she could manage while the gunman began a rant.

"There's something seriously wrong with those things! Those fuckers have ruined my life. And others'. I know they have! But no one understands; no one believes or pays attention. They just look the other way while the people who make this shit keep doing it. They . . ."

The gunman started to cry just as Maisie dropped some of the boxes. She ducked down onto her haunches and picked them up again, then went for the ones on the lower shelves. She spared glances up to him as she grabbed; he paced nervously about the aisle, the gun aimed lazily at the floor.

"The same shit happened to my cousin. *And* a college buddy. They went to the hospital, got checked out, ran tests—but the doctors couldn't explain it. I went when it started happening to me, and they couldn't help me, either. Asked if we'd been out of the country, or if we were exposed to something. Radiation, or some shit like that—fucked if I know. But we hadn't been. No way. So they asked if we were allergic to anything."

The gunman gave a humorless laugh and reached a hand up to his mask. "Does this look like a fucking allergic reaction to you?"

He pulled the mask off, revealing scruffy black hair and a round, red face. And not just red—practically scarlet, the bulge of his cheeks and folds of his forehead livid with the color. His ears, nose, and lips were puffy and raw, and while Maisie had seen similar swellings from allergies, this seemed incredibly extreme. The whole effect made his head look like a balloon filled with blood—a balloon on the verge of bursting.

Maisie turned away, not wanting to get too good of a look at him, should he realize that his hostage could now identify him—and besides, he wasn't exactly pleasant to look at..

She kept grabbing at the Little Devils as the man continued on with his crazy explanation.

"Then my doctor asked what I'd been eating lately. Said maybe I had something that didn't agree with me. *I'd say so*. It was these god damn snack cakes. I just know it was!"

He kicked out at a box which just slipped from Maisie's grasp, sending it flying to the end of the aisle. She whimpered but kept on with the task, her arms nearly full now, the corner of a Big Bad Boy box jabbing up into her neck.

"I'd just started eating them when this began happening to me. And my cousin and buddy had done the same. Gina tried them a few weeks before, and Tyler just one or so. And then when Gina—"

The gunman stopped as his stomach gurgled and churned again. He groaned in pain and set his hands to his knees, huffing as his gut eased itself once more. When he spoke again, it was through more tears.

"And then Tyler a few days later. It was awful! No one knew how it happened. No one realized it's these fucking cakes that caused it. I told them, but no one believed me. Sure, it sounds crazy, but you know what's crazier?"

The man reached his free hand into his pocket and brought out a phone. He thumbed it and stepped over to Maisie as she stood up with her haul. He shoved the phone in her face, showing her a picture of some guy. He held a beer in his hand and was smiling wide. He was probably about her age. Lean, thin-faced, not entirely handsome, but definitely decent. He had scruffy black hair and was wearing a very baggy jersey with a . . .

Maisie gawked at the photo, not sure if she could believe her eyes.

"Yeah, that's me," the gunman said. "From just *two weeks* ago."

He flicked his phone off and returned it to his jeans. While raising the gun, he waddled back and away from Maisie.

"Those fucking cakes did this to me and my friends. I don't know how, but they did. And if no one can or is gonna help us, I will at least try and stop it from happening to others. We're gonna burn all that you've got, here and in the back, and you can *never* sell these things again! And then I'm gonna—"

Another grumble from his stomach sounded off like distant

thunder. The man doubled over again, his arms wrapping around his belly as he screamed in pain.

"Shit! No! It's happening. God, no . . . "

He looked up to Maisie and started panting, jabbing one of his sausage fingers toward her. He seemed to be growing redder by the second—was it just the light playing tricks, or was his face actually . . . *getting bigger*?

"You have to get rid of those, no matter wha!" the man cried. "Burn them! Stop people from eat—"

A shrill yell cut into his plea as his spine arched, his whole body going rigid with a spasm of agony. Maisie screamed and took a step back, realizing that, yes, he *was* indeed getting larger. His fingers were puffing up; his neck was spilling out of his jersey like a cake rising in an oven; his raw belly was peeking out over his jeans; and she could even hear the fabric of his clothes tearing and bones snapping as he continued to expand.

He screamed again, and Maisie joined him. Then his jersey and jacket ripped open—and so did he.

His skin and fat separated from the bones until the pressure was simply too much to withstand. As the remaining flesh split, the gunman exploded like a piñata of blood, torn clothes, and meat morsels. A stream of red splashed over the tiled floor, along the aisle—and saturated Maisie. Her scream altered into a choked gag as she felt the man's warm, sticky blood wash over her arms and face like a wave. Bits of bone-shrapnel pelted the boxes she held and fleshy chunks entangled themselves in her auburn hair.

Maisie stood there a moment, frozen and horrified, watching as a scarlet mist dissipated in the air.

As the meaty *pop* of the man rang itself out of her ears, she let the splattered Little Devils fall to the floor. Shaking her arms, she tried desperately to rid herself of the blood as another scream rose up in her.

Maisie ran, leaping over the pile of soaked clothes and jumbled human remains, her sneakers squeaking along the slick floor. She bolted for the exit, flinging open the doors as she went screaming into the parking lot.

The Dollar Stop grew quiet again, save for the *drip-drip-drip* of ruined items in aisle six, and the Little Devils the man wanted to destroy lied soggy and ruined in the seeping pools of his blood.

GRINDER

Nikki Noir

GHOST WAS ONLY half-aware of the dust clouds blowing past the window as Dean drove. She wasn't seeing the desert or thinking about business; she was imagining a tropical island resort. She let the rumble of the tires lull her further into the daydream. Her senses drifted, and the sound of the highway melted into a new background of exotic birds chirping and the rushing of fresh, blue waterfalls. The sun was warm, and the breeze was cool. One day soon this wouldn't be just a daydream; it would be the reward Dean had promised her for all their hard work.

She'd climbed onto the back of Dean's motorcycle the day senior year ended, didn't even make it to the graduation ceremony. Everyone in the small town of Sierra Vista knew Dean made his money buying and selling drugs, but Ghost didn't care. She felt alive and safe with him. And after three years of hustlin' together, they were finally reaching their bankroll goal.

The car slowed, and when the crunching gravel stopped, Ghost opened her eyes and returned to the present. Rodrigo's large estate loomed; the only structure on this particular strip of desert between Tombstone and Nogales. It was a lovely house and ranch, but Ghost was happy to know this would be their last time visiting. She had nothing against Rodrigo—it was always fun getting high with him— but Dean and her were not true players in the game, even Sonny couldn't compete. For Rodrigo the game was life. For them it was just a means to an end—that exotic life she fantasied about each day.

Ghost looked at Dean. His forearm flexed as he turned off the engine, and the familiar warm ache returned to her pelvis. That feeling had helped her continue the lifestyle these last three years. It was the power and money about the deals that turned Ghost on. Not the drugs. Smoking weed was fun to a point, but she could it at a moment's notice. Long as the money and power remained in their lives.

Ghost looked to the back seat at the same time Sonny passed the duffel bag forward to Dean.

"Double check my math," Sonny said. Then Ghost watched his eyes move to her, there was a hunger in his gaze.

Sonny's attention further fueled the buzzing warmth in her crotch and she held his gaze for a long second before looking away. Ghost didn't feel the least bit guilty about sending Sonny a few vibes of false hope. It was that power trip again. She smiled, wondering what Sonny would give to be a part of their post-deal celebration. Then she wondered if they'd even still hang out with Sonny after their days of dealing were over. They'd always worked as a trio. But from day one, Dean had introduced her to Sonny as his business partner, and it always seemed more like a loyal business partnership for them rather than a true friendship.

She watched Dean's muscles as he sorted through the money in the bag. "Looks good to me," Dean said, passing the bag back. "Remember. Nothing changes. We don't mention our retirement. This is just another exchange as always. Right?"

"Right," said Sonny.

"Yes, sir." Ghost smiled, almost calling him daddy. She was getting a little caught up in the excitement. It felt dirty to use that word and there was certainly no redeeming qualities about her own father, but for some reason with Dean it felt okay to be a little dirty. He was their leader, and oh boy did she loved watching the father of their trio take control in situations.

"All right then," Dean said. "Let's do this."

As always, they sat on three couches arranged in a loose triangle around a large wood and glass coffee table. Rodrigo on one couch,

Dean and Sonny on the second, and Ghost on the third. The large living room, as usual, reeked of smoke and alcohol, but tonight the potent aroma smelled different. More like incense than drug smoke. That would change soon, she figured, watching Rodrigo light up a blunt.

Rodrigo took two deep drags. "We didn't have stuff like this when I was a kid." He released a thick cloud. "Cross bred to twenty percent THC nowadays."

"Potent as fuck." Sonny laughed and Ghost could see him eyeing the blunt similar to how he'd looked at her in the car.

Rodrigo nodded. "Twenty percent ain't shit anymore though. Dispensaries are on our fucking asses with medical grade. Thirty percent THC and probably higher." He drew a third puff and held it as he passed the blunt to Dean. "We need to up our game."

Dean accepted and took a small hit, which was the signal that Sonny and her could also both partake if they wanted. "Well, our customers are happy with the product. Is the deal not working for you anymore?"

"No, it's working . . . " Then Rodrigo's eyes got a sparkle to them and he leaned forward. "But what if I got my hands on something really big? What if you could pocket ten times what you're making now. Would you be interested?"

Dean passed the blunt to Sonny who was near drooling when it got to him. Dean looked to Ghost; she wasn't sure what to do, so she nodded. If this was the finale, a little extra money wouldn't hurt.

"Yeah. We'd be down," Dean said. "What's the product?"

Rodrigo laughed a bit. "*Amoladora*. Means Grinder. And it's . . . How to describe it . . . ?" His eyes took on a glaze.

Sonny let loose a cloud of thick smoke and passed the blunt to Ghost. She held the smoking wrap. It was definitely weed, but there was something else, just below the skunky green smell. Though she couldn't identify the odor, it reminded her of the first time she'd met Rodrigo. The first time she'd sat on this couch and got high on the weed and the rush of watching Dean work. The only thing missing was Lupita, Rodrigo's woman. She was usually here. Now that Ghost thought of it, there were usually the bodyguards too, back near the kitchen. Everyone was missing today.

Ghost took a deep puff, holding the smoke, until her chest

burned. Upon exhaling, her tits tingled and burned as warmth raided from her heart. It took a moment to steady herself, before handing the blunt back to Rodrigo. He accepted it although he still seemed deep in thought.

Damn that hit hard, Ghost thought.

"Grinder is like nothing you've seen before," Rodrigo said. "Ecstasy. Molly. Nothing comes close. It's powerful. One must be careful—"

A chorus of moans floated down the staircase. Ghost had never heard Lupita's sex voice, but she felt positive that it was Rodrigo's woman upstairs who was responsible for the cries of pleasure.

"Very powerful." A grin spread across Rodrigo's tan face, exposing several gold teeth. "What can I say, we got a little greedy, tested it out."

Ghost felt a flush sweep over her body. She flashed a look at Dean. This must be how Sonny had felt the day he'd caught a glimpse of Ghost going down on Dean in the front seat. That had been the day she'd gotten super high and super horny after a big transaction. That day was the reason why Sonny now gave her the hungry eyes.

Rodrigo tapped the blunt's ash on the wooden table, seemingly oblivious to the fact there was no ashtray. Then, from his shirt pocket he retrieved a small vial and placed it on the table. Ghost stared at the vial of red liquid.

"So it's like MDMA?" Dean asked, studying the vial. "What's the active ingredient?"

"In Sonora, there's a toad. Its glands spray DMT for defense—"

"That's where the whole toad licking thing came from?" Sonny's eyes now looked at the vial with the same intensity he'd eyed the blunt with.

Rodrigo nodded.

"So Grinder is a form of animal poison?" Dean asked.

The stairs creaked and soft footsteps padded down. Lupita appeared, staggering to the couch in a sundress, her hair tousled, her small feet shoeless. She stopped with a jerk and sat close to Ghost. Her body smelled like sex.

"Not exactly animal poison." Rodrigo leaned over and gave the blunt to Lupita. "Like DMT, Grinder can be made with the aid of living organisms. It was a secret I . . . recently acquired."

Lupita let loose a cloud and Ghost noticed that everyone's gaze had shifted to her. In that moment, she also became aware that her head was floating in a way it hadn't in years. Her heart was racing.
Shit!

She wasn't just buzzing; she was fucking stoned. Too stoned. They all were. Even Rodrigo now that she analyzed it. Everyone was disjointed, and she was positive that they were all moving at half-speed.
Or am I just being paranoid?

After a puff, Lupita stood shakily and offered the weed to Dean. Dean leaned back and declined with a wave of his hand. He must have noticed it too.
He's trying to sober up.

This had never happened before on a deal. A good buzz yes, but not this kind of high. Everyone was acting so weird. Lupita was sporting 'sex' hair' and Rodrigo was being sketchy with his new product pitch.

"That small bottle . . . " Rodrigo pointed to the tiny red vial on the table. "You can make a grand from that alone."

"A grand? From that?"

"*Si*. One drop and it's an aphrodisiac. Two drops and you'll hump anything that moves." Rodrigo erupted in laughter. When he quieted, his face grew a bit somber. "Never do more than two drops. There was a reason *they* kept it a secret." He looked to Lupita who was back on the sofa but shifting restlessly.

Ghost tried to focus on her breathing, but something in her stomach and chest fought for her attention. A blooming heat with a warmth that was triple what she had felt before swelled in her core. The electric warmth branched out, crawling its way both up into her ears and down into her loins.

"Come." Rodrigo rose at a snail's pace. He steadied himself before stepping out of the triangle of couches. "Let me show you."

Dean stood but his moves were jerky and Ghost could tell he was fighting to keep his composure. Sonny followed next, moving just as strained.

"You stay with Lupita." Rodrigo looked to Ghost.

"Sure," Ghost stammered, not sure why she felt scared.

Ghost felt Lupita's hand on her thigh. "Bueno," the woman whispered.

Ghost tried to keep the anxiety from her face.

"Okay. It's in the basement." Rodrigo pointed across the room to an open door at the north end of the house.

"Lead the way," Dean said.

The men left, and Ghost felt Lupita's weight shift as the woman leaned closer. Ghost stared at the caramel-colored skin and manicured nails of Lupita's thin hand.

"Shhh." Lupita stroked her leg.

Ghost took deep breaths, allowing Lupita's touch to calm her. When she opened her eyes, the anxiety was gone. And oddly, as she stared at the woman's hand, Ghost found herself wondering how Lupita took such good care of herself while Rodrigo was a bit of a slob. When Lupita's delicate hand began massaging her thigh harder, the electricity it created in her body hindered further productive thought. Her last realization was that this drug deal had gotten very strange. Nothing like this had ever happened in the past. They smoked, bullshitted for a minute, and then left with the goods. Always. Yet Ghost ignored the questions this turn of events caused and allowed herself to focus on the electric waves that traveled through her jeans and into her pussy instead.

So weird . . . but so nice.

A part of Ghost wanted to push Lupita's hand away, but instead she closed her eyes and that part of her struggling to resist fell further from her mind. In her memory, Ghost replayed the incident with Sonny in the car again. They'd just flipped a shipment for five thousand. And they knew it wouldn't be long until they had the final ten thousand needed to invest in legal real estate. It'd been their biggest score to date and Dean had pulled over before they even got home and double-checked the bag. After seeing the money, mixed with the weed buzz she had going, Ghost had lost her head a bit that day. She'd forgotten all about Sonny in the backseat.

To Ghost, it was just her and Dean. She had slid the duffel bag aside and reached for his pants. Dean hadn't attempted to stop her. She smiled, tugging down his pants, and bringing his cock into view. She'd enjoyed his flesh for a good minute before she heard the audible swallowing and shifting in the back seat. She looked back to see Sonny, jaw slack, eyes wide, staring over the seat at them.

Whoops.

Instead of embarrassment, it'd given her a surge of power. She took her time sliding her lips off Dean's erection, wiping away a strand of saliva while giving Sonny a succubus grin—

"Ghost . . . "

The soft voice broke her through her memory. Ghost opened her eyes and felt the warmth of Lupita's fingertips against her lips. "I see why they call you that. Your skin is so smooth and so pale."

Ghost swallowed hard. This was wrong. Very wrong. She was being pulled deep into Lupita's green almond eyes. *This weed is tainted!* That was the only explanation.

"What's happening?"

"Something wonderful. Can't you feel it?" Lupita's hands slipped from Ghost's lips and slid down her neck and across the left strap of her tank top. Lupita turned her fingers so her shiny red nails scraped lightly down Ghost's arm. "Come upstairs. Bruno is upstairs."

She gripped Ghost's hand.

Ghost opened her mouth, but the words wouldn't fall out. "N-n-n . . . " Ghost shook her head while a million emotions bubbled up inside her. She was still aware of Dean, of the job they had to finish.

"Please. I want to show you. Bruno and I have something to give you." Lupita stood, swaying slightly.

Ghost allowed herself to be pulled up from the couch, the crotch of her jeans soaked with heat. "Lupita . . . think about Rodrigo. Dean . . . " Her voice was losing strength. She knew something was wrong. Maybe this was Grinder, but why had they drugged them with an ecstasy-like substance? For sex? Rodrigo and Lupita were a power couple, but never presented themselves as swingers.

Without answers, and not enough willpower to say no, Ghost was dragged forward and up the stairs. Lupita held her hands, trying to walk backward, stumbling often. Ghost's eyes transfixed on her bouncing cleavage heaving against the low cut of her sundress. Halfway up the steps Ghost hated herself for losing control. This must be how a sex addict feels. Every fiber craving lust. Needing to orgasm for the sheer sake of orgasm.

Ghost found her voice somehow. "Why did you drug us?"

"We'd never get you in bed otherwise." Her eyes flashed. "We need you."

They were across the landing now and Lupita just laughed,

delirious. She opened the door to the first bedroom on the left and yanked Ghost inside. Ghost almost fell, steadying herself first against Lupita, then pulling away when she found herself wanting to bury her face into the woman's full breasts, like some male teenage horndog. She looked around the lavished room trying to shake the feel of Lupita's hard nipples that had poked into Ghost's own tits when Lupita caught her.

"I'll watch but that's all." Saying it out loud helped reassure her mentally.

A love sofa sat a few feet from an enormous four-post bed. Carved of elegant dark wood, the white bedding was a bright contrast against it. The sofa was white too, and the floor was a black-stained hardwood. A few paintings—gothic almost, like they belonged in a castle—filled the walls.

As Ghost calmed herself, her eyes focused on the sofa, noticing Bruno the bodyguard for the first time. It was jarring to see him naked except for his gun shoulder-holster. He held a huge cock at attention and was slowly rubbing it as Lupita pushed Ghost closer.

Ghost pushed back, resisting Lupita's playful prodding.

Lupita giggled. "Okay. Have it your way. Just watch. For now . . . " And with that, she walked past Ghost and dropped her sun dress about her ankles. She stepped out revealing a toned and beautifully light brown body. Her breasts fit her body perfectly, larger than average, but not too big. Erect nipples popped up from large dark areola.

Ghost watched Lupita tie back her dark hair, then prance over to Bruno. She flashed a devilish smile then sunk to her knees and began sucking the tip of Bruno's large cock. Lupita eyed Ghost as she sucked, and a charge went through her. This must be how Dean felt when he watched Ghost go down on him. Or perhaps it was more like how Sonny was feeling that day in the backseat. Like a dirty voyeur, a fly on the wall, Ghost stared. This was beyond watching a porno. This was real life. It was people she knew.

Before realizing it, Ghost had her pants unbuttoned and two fingers deep inside her wet pussy as she watched them.

Dean was halfway down the basement stairs, and already he knew he was in trouble. He just didn't know how bad it was yet. He'd watched Rodrigo puff on the same blunt as he had, so it couldn't be laced with poison. Which meant it was just super potent weed. That was all. He needed to chill the fuck out. Dean held the banister to steady himself as they entered the basement.

He tried to mask the spacey confusion in his head and remind himself that he'd been in this basement before. Nothing weird was gonna happen to him or Sonny. Then he saw the form—

"Jesus Christ, Rodrigo! Is that Ivan?"

Rodrigo sighed, turned slowly and nodded. "I'm finding Grinder is not something to play with." He gestured to the naked figure that hung from the thick western-style beams running the length of the basement ceiling. A red rope was around the naked man's neck. "Too late for Ivan now. Too late for all of them I think." Rodrigo's eyes looked mad, his laugh was breathy. "You though . . . you're both okay. Come. I must show you."

Dean felt Sonny's hand on his shoulder. "I don't feel right. What the fuck did he do to us?" Sonny's voice trembled. "You hear me, Rodrigo?"

"Sonny. Cool it," Dean whispered.

"Fuck that. There's a dead guy hanging from the ceiling and he's acting like it's no big deal!"

Sonny advanced, but Dean grabbed his arm. "Enough."

Dean wanted to run too, but his body seemed to move to the will of someone else, *something* else. He found himself moving forward, drawn as if by the Pied Piper. Dean took a wide path around the swaying figure that had once been a bodyguard. Despite the distance he tried to achieve, Dean couldn't pull his eyes away from Ivan's purple face. The man's dick was still erect, and a wet spot stained the floor below him. A chair was toppled over a few feet away. It looked more like a sex act gone wrong, than a suicide.

"Fuck that," Sonny said.

Dean looked back and Sonny was sitting on the ground.

"I'm not going anywhere. I feel like . . . like. I can't . . . " Sonny started rubbing his crotch.

One drop is an aphrodisiac. Two drops and you'll hump

anything that moves, Dean remembered Rodrigo's description of Grinder.

"What *did* you do to us, Rodrigo?"

"I am making you a part of history." Rodrigo smiled. "This is the future of the drug trade. Be honest, do you not love the sensation it gives you?"

"You did drug us! What the fuck, Rodrigo!"

Rodrigo raised his hands, calmly, then he gestured to the open door behind him, the only room in the basement. "Come now. I can explain."

Dean's gut was telling him to run, to fight the ecstasy pulsing through his body. To maintain and not give into animal lust.

"I need your help. We keep it in the dungeon. It felt most appropriate."

Ghost leaned against the door frame, breathing heavy, as she caressed her wet slit. She watched Lupita leave thick globs of spit on Bruno's impressive cock, then stand up and turn her back to him. Ghost met her gaze and maintained contact as Lupita sat back on Bruno. She brought her feet up to the couch cushions and hovered over Bruno's engorged member. She took hold of the stiff rod and slowly lowered her ass. Lupita guided Bruno, sliding him into her tight hole. Neither woman broke the stare and Ghost could sense Lupita's ecstasy as she finally sat flush against Bruno's lap, her asshole having taken his entire length. Ghost breathed in time with the expressions of pain and pleasure that rolled over Lupita's face.

Lupita leaned further back against Bruno and looked down, watching his cock penetrate her ass as she fingered herself. Ghost continued to stare as Lupita slapped and rubbed her short brown pussy lips. A vibrating moan emanated from Lupita's throat and Ghost saw the woman's face flush. Then her head snapped up and Lupita stared into Ghost's eyes. She lifted a finger, wet with pussy juice, and beckoned to Ghost.

Ghost's shook her head no. Yet despite the refusal, somehow, she was moving like mist over the hardwood floor toward them anyway.

The wood was hard on her knees when she lowered herself and crawled between Bruno's legs. She could smell the musky scent of his sweaty skin and was mesmerized this close up by Bruno's fat meat pole sinking in then out of Lupita's ass.

Lupita spread her pussy lips and beckoned Ghost again. Ghost could imagine the hot wet folds of Lupita's vagina against her mouth, but she couldn't actually make it happen. This was crazy. Where was Dean? Her head was airy; what if she was hallucinating right now?

"Please," Lupita said, rubbing her clit, continuing to open and close her pink hole.

Ghost leaned forward on her hands and knees but hesitated again.

"Please." Lupita's voice built in volume. She was now throwing herself down against Bruno's lap, impaling her ass on his cock. Drool started to form at her mouth as her body convulsed. Something dark filled the puckering opening of her vagina. Ghost gasped, her own legs wobbled, and she started to back away.

"Ohh . . . Please . . ." Lupita shook wildly and let loose a massive wail.

A fountain of orgasmic fluid shot from under her clit, splashing against the wood floor. Ghost scrambled away as the fluid slid toward her. Meanwhile, Lupita collapsed onto Bruno's stomach.

Ghost had never seen a woman squirt before and while she didn't want to get her face drenched, she still marveled at how Lupita had reached a level of total ecstasy, seemingly losing all control of her muscles, squirting like a man.

Despite her initial fear, the sight now made her hot again. Bruno was still pounding away, and Lupita shook like a rag doll. Ghost closed her eyes and explored herself again. Then Bruno grunted loudly. Ghost opened her eyes when she heard Lupita hit the floor. The woman fell into her own orgasmic puddle of ejaculate and piss.

My God, she orgasmed herself into unconsciousness.

That's when Ghost saw some*thing* on the floor sliding back toward Lupita's vagina.

Ghost felt queasy, all ecstasy had momentarily left her. What the fuck was that thing? Had it sprayed out of Lupita? Ghost felt helpless to look away from the pink tumor-looking tissue, a piece of animated meat. Scrunching up its wrinkled body, it inched forward like a demented worm.

She pushed it out when she squirted! That thing was inside her and she was gonna spray it into my mouth. Now it's trying to return to her pussy before it dies! It sounded crazy, but that was how the puzzle seemed to be assembling itself inside Ghost's drugged-out mind.

Fighting the haze, Ghost buttoned her pants and pushed her hair back, then took one last look. The squishy organ was now pushing against Lupita's labia. Lupita herself remained unconscious. Ghost's gaze found Bruno, sitting on the couch, panting hard, a frantic look in his eyes. He stroked his cock, staring back at Ghost. Then he came, and streams of cum dribbled out of his mushroom tip.

Bruno grunted, but it sounded more pained than pleased. He smeared the semen across his chest and went right back to jerking his cock. A disgusted look of compulsion filled his face, but he didn't stop stroking. Ghost looked down at her wet fingers and smelt her sex. She knew what he was feeling. She'd succumbed to it too, an uncontrollable sexual force.

And that thing! How was that creature *involved? Why had they tried to infect her with it?*

She glanced again and the tumor-looking organism was gone.

"Aggghhh." Bruno must have climaxed again. She turned back to him but saw no semen this time. It was as if his pipes had been drained of cum though his libido had not diminished. He staggered to his feet and Ghost ran into the hallway, slamming the door shut.

"Dean!" She bolted toward the basement door.

Dean could taste the sickly-sweet aroma curling out from the open door, pulling him inward. The same incense as the blunt Rodrigo had passed around. Dean followed him into the room he had called the 'dungeon'. The scent in the air seemed to intensify his intoxication. It was cool inside the room, a pleasing contrast to the fire that had made its way into his crotch.

Dean walked past a sex swing and a large chase lounge with handcuffs attached to the frame. Dean had never seen Rodrigo and Lupita as sex freaks, but he wasn't surprised. Everyone was a freak in one way or another. No wonder Grinder hit them so hard. Their day to day life was a fetish, so Grinder must had accidentally turned them into sex lunatics for the moment.

"What's that?" Dean's heavy eyes struggled to focus on the form at the far end of the room.

"*Mirra. Mirra.*" Rodrigo was next to him now, and Dean felt himself moving with the man, closer and closer to the St. Andre's Cross at the far end of the dungeon.

There was a woman bound to the cross, nude except for a leather mask over her face. Her legs were strapped to the bottom of the cross. Her arms, instead of being fixed to the upper wood of the cross, hung at her side. Cuffs around both wrists attached to the floor of the contraption by long chains.

Dean looked to Rodrigo, he offered nothing but a dopey smile. He turned back to the figure. Long IV tubing stretched from insertions in the crook of both elbows down to two glass jars that were filling with the what looked like blood. Two more IV tubes ran from both legs into an additional two jars. They were draining her of blood. The body was trembling.

Dean remembered the red liquid, the vial of Grinder Rodrigo had shown them. "What the fuck is this?" He snapped from the lethargy and spun around. His stomach dropped when he saw Rodrigo pointing a 9mm at him.

"I fucked up," Rodrigo said, his tone emotionless, detached from the chaos around him. "I gave them all too much. I didn't respect the *amoladora.*" He shrugged, keeping the gun trained on Dean.

Dean raised his hands. "Come on, man, it's me, Dean. Put the gun down. You're fucking high."

Rodrigo stepped up to the chained woman, placed his free hand on her abdomen that seemed slightly bulged as compared to the thinness of the rest of her body. Rodrigo caressed the bump in her flesh. "By the time I found the optimal dosage it was too late for them. Relax. That was a few days ago. What you and I smoked was okay. I measured it perfectly. Once I sober up, I'll start the new empire."

"They've been like this for a couple days!"

"Damn near mindless nymphomaniacs. They're bodies are too damaged to support a*moladora.*"

Dean looked back to the IVs bloodletting the woman and saw that the flow was slowing to a drip into the mason jars.

"Lupita and I were going to rule it all. Wanted your crew to be the runners and we'd just used street trash as hosts. Hobos and hookers. But if Lupita and Bruno die, I'll have no fresh bodies to transfer the organ into. The venture will die before it ever gets started."

"Fuck!" Dean jumped as the bulge in the woman's stomach moved. The bubble of flesh began inching upward. It moved like an animal burrowing through the dirt. The form disappeared between her large breasts, then reappeared shortly later at the base of the woman's neck.

Dean felt paralyzed watching the progression of the anomaly. A part of his brain screamed to run away, but he couldn't command his feet to move. Besides, he couldn't outrun a bullet.

Rodrigo undid the leather mask on the woman's face, alternating his attention between the leather lacing and Dean, the gun hovering level with Dean's chest.

"Again. I didn't want it to go down this way. I gave too big a dose. I fucked up." He shook his head as if he had failed in his mission. "But we can't let *amoladora* perish. Can we? It won't let itself perish."

Dean watched him pull the leather mask from the woman. Her head snapped back and her jaws popped open. There was a horrible wrenching noise as bones popped. The woman's mouth unhinged with a tear and gaped open, flesh splitting at the corners. A pink blog of parasitic organ tissue poked out past her teeth. The woman gurgled blood around the creature.

Dean screamed. "What the fuck is that!"

"That is where *amoladora* comes from. The toad as your friend said." Rodrigo smiled watching the fleshy parasitic organism breach higher into the air. Then he took the creature in his left hand and lifted it from the now dead woman. Rodrigo turned to Dean, cradling the monstrosity with one hand, and pointing the gun with the other. "It needs a new host. We can do it the hard way or the easy way." Rodrigo stepped toward him. "Help me. Help us. I won't fuck up again."

Dean heard the crack of bone and Rodrigo's eyes went wide.

Then his head rolled forward and he collapsed to the ground, gun and parasite sliding across the floor. Standing in his place was Ghost, a thick studded paddle in her hands. Dean dropped to his knees and retrieved the gun with a trembling hand.

Ghost ran to him.

"Is he dead?" she asked, gripping Dean around his waist.

Rodrigo moaned and writhed on the floor, and Dean thought about what would happen when everyone sobered. There was no going back. He raised the gun and shot Rodrigo three times in the torso.

Rodrigo's eyes burst open as the bullets tore into his flesh. With glossed eyes the man ripped the buttons off his dress shirt and pulled it open. He began rubbing himself all over, using the blood seeping from his wounds, spreading it up his neck then down inside his pants. Dean did a quick search of the floor but saw no sign of the Grinder. Rodrigo moaned louder, continuing to dip his hands into the bloody bullet holes and rubbing himself harder and harder. With a final scream of pained pleasure, his body went limp.

"He's dead now," Dean said.

"Will *we* be okay?" Ghost asked.

"Yes. This high will pass. We just need . . . time."

"What the hell is all this?" Ghost looked at the woman and the blood jars.

Dean shook his head. "Some kind of parasite that creates a by-product of liquid ecstasy when mixed with human blood." He shook his head and looked down at Rodrigo who was motionless in a pool of blood. "Guess there's a reason it's kept hidden to just the highest cartels." He sighed.

"Guess what else . . . it's all ours," she whispered in Dean's ear. "Once we sober up, we're rich."

"Where's Lupita?" Dean asked.

"Unconscious upstairs." Ghost paused. "She might be dead. *It* was . . . in her."

"There are more of these . . . *things* crawling around.

Ghost nodded.

"Isn't there another bodyguard too . . . Bruno?" Dean asked.

Ghost tried to remember Bruno, but, now that the immediate danger had passed, she was flushing with excitement again. Ghost pushed her finger against his lips. "We'll talk about Bruno later."

Dean stopped protesting and footsteps caught his attention. Sonny approached them.

Ghost no longer felt anxious. Despite everything she'd seen. The threat felt like it was over, and she didn't mind Sonny as he pressed himself into her embrace with Dean. She leaned closer to Dean and breathed in his musk, closing her eyes in passion between the two warm bodies. She exhaled, opened her eyes and gazed upon the bottles of Grinder blood beneath the dead host. Hope surged within her numb brain and she knew they had struck it big.

She had a feeling they'd never use Grinder for their personal use again. Just business. But if they were stuck riding out the high, there was no reason not to enjoy it. Ghost smiled, relishing in the heat and pressure of being sandwiched between Daddy and Sonny. She could feel Sonny's excitement pushing against her ass. After all that teasing, maybe it was time she let him play. After all, this was their final deal. It was over now.

Ghost planted her right hand on Dean's crotch, then reached behind her and grabbed Sonny's with her left. Yes, Sonny had been a good boy. Time for his reward. She'd never wanted a threesome before, but now she couldn't wait to experience a meat triangle. Three as one.

As they ravished her, Ghost forgot about Ivan hanging in the other room, Lupita who may have been in a coma or dead, the blood-drained female host on the St. Andrews Cross, and the missing parasites. The last shred of her rational mind instead thought of Bruno. Maybe he would show up. Then she could have every hole filled at once. What a powerful rush that would be.

I HANG MY HAT AND THERE'S NO BLOOD

ROBERT ESSIG

I WALK INSIDE my condo, hang my hat on the coat rack, and there's no blood.

The condo is behind the Cosmopolitan on the Las Vegas strip. Sounds glamorous, right? Fuck no. It was nice when I bought the place, back when my show was a hit and I was pulling in greenbacks like Liberace performing at a Pride Parade, but those days are long over, not only for the Cosmo, but for me too. You know, I once had girls waiting for me in my dressing room after a show. You wouldn't believe it. Not a guy like me. I'm fat—I can admit it. I'm a fucking comedian! You kidding me? Half my schtick is fat jokes. That's how I got my break.

Anyway, yeah, I live in that condo behind what once was one of the most glamorous casinos on the strip. I once was the comedy hitman of MGM, right up there with the biggies.

After hanging my hat, I slink into my well-worn sofa, pick up the remote and feed my brain with monotonous garbage television. Anything, reality shows, 24-hour news programs, reruns of comedies that are only funny because my life has become one big joke. I don't drown myself in booze, not tonight, and I'll never forgive myself for that. Maybe things would have been different. Probably not, though, fate being what it is.

I wake up the following day, sweating from the heat created by sleeping in the crook of an old couch. I have a bed, but I don't seem to make it into the bedroom before the hypnotic drone of late night television pulls me under. I smell like two-day sweat, like someone deep into a bad flu, but deodorant is to little avail, considering how fucking hot Vegas is in August. 115°F yesterday; 118°F today.

I try to convince myself that I am thankful for the gig I have at the Burt Challenger Theater, a shitty little joint hidden down an alleyway next to a twenty-four hour Indian buffet and a sleazy tourist trap strip mall that doesn't scoff at selling cell phone chargers for twenty bucks a pop, but don't worry, you can get a tallboy for a buck! I loath the place and the help feels about the same toward me. Locals know me by name recognition, but tourists don't remember anyone who's been here as long as I have except for Penn and Teller and Carrottop. P and T have been regulars at the Rio for years. Their mugs, larger than life, can be seen from the I-15. I've completely lost track of ol' Carrot Juice. Maybe someone finally ran his ass out of town.

In front of the MGM Grand there's this giant screen that can be seen a mile down the strip in either direction. Ten years ago, I ruled that screen. My show was one of the most popular comedy shows on the strip. I was told I had done so well for MGM in such a short time that I was basically a living Vegas legend. I saw a street named after me like the guys in the Rat Pack, I saw the theater I performed in being named after me, but more importantly I saw money, enough of the stuff to not have to worry about a thing until the day I croaked.

I've learned that people say a lot of things. People use words like tiny weapons in some sick mental cold war. String them together one way and you melt someone's heart, you feed an ego; take those same words, twist them a bit, and they turn into daggers.

There's a lot on my mind, too much to focus. I don't do much to prepare myself for the show, not here at the condo. The walk to the Burt Challenger Theater reduces me to a pile of sweaty biscuit dough. I hate the walk. Every goddamn day.

So much on my mind. Like the woman in the audience last night. I haven't seen her before. She . . . well, it's not like I have fans anymore. Even the most loyal ones from the good ol' days have long forgotten me. It isn't that I don't get a decent crowd, I do, it's just the people are getting their tickets for free from associated casinos or buying them at a crazy reduction on various third-party websites.

I know this, and I know the theater is hoping they stop by the little souvenir display and buy a shirt with my name and a pathetically generic public domain image of a deck of cards. I don't even understand it. My show has nothing to do with cards.

I hit the muggy streets a good two and a half hours before my show starts. My nostrils are assaulted by the smells of garbage, car exhaust, cigars, and the unmistakable rank of a sewer system that's either over capacitated or overheated from a string of forty-five straight days of one-hundred-plus degree weather. That's the worst of it, the shit smell. You don't ever get used to it, and sometimes it creeps into the hallways of the condo. As you walk the perpetually busy streets you can feel the smells as they hit you in tiny bursts like invisible raunchy beings there to set your ass straight. Kids ask if I want to buy coke, weed, pills, and I ignore them today and everyday as I walk across Las Vegas Boulevard on a bridge above the constant three and a half mile per hour traffic below.

On the other side of the bridge, the streets are always thick with a mix of lemming tourists and street performers in varied degrees of despair. The young girls wear pasties and a g-string, dancing to the latest misogynist hip-hop tunes, accepting donations for a photograph. The newer magicians have more elaborate setups, still filled with some kind of hope that won't last. The ones who have been there longer than maybe six months look like sad clowns without makeup, practically begging for someone to pick a card, any card. And then there are the homeless, hairy, dirty, and skeletal— they look like middle-aged Americans in the final dregs of the worst concentration camps of Hitler's Germany.

Those guys used to be magicians, singers, jugglers, dreamers.

I'd love to say you get used to seeing the street performers, but you just don't. They're everywhere these days, on every corner, vying for every one of your dollar bills, and so few of them are worth a penny.

Believe it or not, I got my break as a street comic. Back in those days street performers were the exception to the rule. You pretty much had to have it authorized by the casino if you were taking up real estate, and that meant I had to have a meeting with some manager or whatnot, and I had to convince them that having me outside would encourage people to enter their establishment. That actually turned out to be my in with the once great Imperial Palace, which is now imploded. The place was nicknamed the Venereal Palace due to the amount of college kids who stayed there because of the cheap rooms. I chose to gig outside there since it was close to Caesars, the Flamingo, and Belaggio, amongst other well renowned outfits. Any further west and I might as well make balloon animals in front of Circus Circus.

The crowds I wrangled were so massive that the Imperial Palace figured they had better give me a slot in their theater to bring those folks inside to gamble, and that's how I got my first gig. My schtick has always been a little politics, a little current events, and a lot of self-deprecation. People love that shit. They just love to laugh at someone who has it worse than they do, even though I was eventually doing better than ninety-nine percent of my average audience.

Christ, that was a long time ago.

The Burt Challenger Theater isn't much to behold, and you could walk by the alley five times looking for the place. I slip in the front door and show myself to the backstage area, pretending that Denise and Sal didn't give me a double dose of the evil eye like the future of their livelihood depended on my next performance.

Maybe it did.

At least the place was air-conditioned. After cooling down and getting ready, I take the stage, curious to see how many people are in the audience. It's an intimate stage with a cluster of cocktail tables in the center of the floor, booths lining the sides, and rows of seating in the back. I'm only surprised by the turnout because that's what I'm supposed to feel. There are at least double the amount of people as usual, but the same as yesterday.

My stage setup is rather simple. I have a stool in case I need to take a breather or my legs get to me. On the stool is a highball glass of apple juice. People like to believe I'm an alky who feels the necessity to drink-up while on stage. Nope. I just need something to wet my whistle every so many jokes. Next to the stool is a bag of props. Don't judge. Prop comedy pretty much died in the early nineties, but I like to mix it into my show. Ol' Carrot Cake made a great career for himself with rubber chickens and the like, so why not?

I HANG MY HAT AND THERE'S NO BLOOD

I start out with a greeting; they clap and genuinely look happy to be there, which is always a plus. I sling a few quick fat jokes. Kids like to get their wings when they fly in an airplane . . . I got my wings too . . . at KFC. I have frequent flier miles at McDonald's. It gets even worse from there, and the smiles start to fade. Self-loathing seeps in, as it does every night when I'm bombing. The tried and true jokes lift them up a bit, but it's to little avail. I just don't have the ability to hold an audience anymore. My knack for writing great material seems to have evaporated in the Vegas heat. Maybe it's that I just don't relate to people any longer, too much time on this hellish strip of casinos and hotels having turned my mind to garbage.

As I stand there, slinging jokes, killing some and bombing others, there's this niggling voice in the back of my head. It's the voice of my boss, Burt Challenger himself (an old magician who opened the theater in his retirement, the lucky bastard). You see, last week he pulled the plug on my show.

On top of that, tonight is my last performance.

You're all washed up. He actually said that to me like we'd time traveled back to black and white era films. He's right, and on such short notice I haven't been able to secure another gig, not even down on Freemont or one of the many casinos sprinkling the outskirts of downtown.

A man can only handle so much rejection before he gives up, and I'm not going back to performing on the streets. I'm too old for that shit. It would kill me before I had a chance to devolve to the state of your common bum.

Halfway through the show, I start pulling props from my bag. Stupid gags that make the right person laugh, the kind of person who likes slapstick. There are a few in the audience, but not enough to create an infectious response. The power of laughter is amazing, really. I've watched people hate the show, just sitting there with their arms crossed over their chest and staring at me like they are daring me to say something funny. Now, that shit used to get the best of me. I knew if I could get the people around that dead fish to laugh uproariously, the laughter would become infectious and soon enough old dead fish would be flopping around, inadvertently having a great time.

Laughter is a great power, but other things are powerful as well.

I pull a shotgun from my prop bag. The audience is quiet, but unflinching. They don't seem to realize the danger they are in, which is good. Fear is as contagious as laughter, if not more so, and it would only take one screamer to tear this place down.

Of course, I keep on joking, pulling from social commentary about gun rights. There have been so many mass shootings that I can joke about it now, particularly since there wasn't one this week . . . yet.

I do jokes about what we'll use old shotguns for after the democrats take our guns away, appeasing to the conservative half of the audience, and then I make fun of redneck crackers shooting off their own toes trying to deal with nasty corns, appeasing the lefties, and then I go into a story joke, really captivating the entire audience. The story is about an old porn star in some retirement home. She mistakes a shotgun for her favorite dildo. I know, I know, sounds fucking stupid as shit, but you had to be there. You'd have been laughing like everyone else. When I'm hot, I can make you laugh at cancer.

I make a show of lying down on my back at the edge of the stage, shotgun in hand and resting on my chest. I tilted my head over the lip of the stage and looked at the audience from a nauseating upside-down vantage, acting like a semi-blind old porn star, which was kind of like a pantomime of Jenna Jameson's reanimated career.

"And then she puts the dildo in her mouth like this . . . " I raise my head so that the audience is getting a solid view of the back of my sweaty, balding dome. I place the barrel of the shotgun in my mouth and make obnoxious sounds, gyrating the gun like I get a kick out of sucking on cobalt steel.

Then I pull the trigger.

The back of my head explodes like the aftermath of putting an M80 in a watermelon. I actually hear their cries of shock in that last moment before I die. It's horrifying. I hear it over and over, ringing through my consciousness like alarm bells and I know what I have done.

They weren't prepared for a splash zone.

I lay there with my head hanging over the edge of the stage, leaking blood and brain patè onto the floor while screams dominate the theater and the smell of gunpowder rises to the rafters.

I HANG MY HAT AND THERE'S NO BLOOD

The first time this happened I think I must have laid there for a half an hour before I got my bearings. By lying there, I can listen to the things that happened in the past, but it's really not all that interesting. Why live in the past? (That's a little inside joke I have with myself.)

I get up. My head feels as big as a hot air balloon and yet there's this cool sensation from the air conditioning blowing on the gaping hole in the back of my cranium. Gives me a chill every time. After pushing the hangers of brain and flesh into the singed, bloody cavity, I find my hat and put it on in a feeble attempt to hide the shame. That's when I look out over the audience.

The new girl is there, the one from yesterday. Looks like maybe she has rope burns on her neck. Sometimes I can't believe what I've wrought. The first time I replayed the final performance, two of the people in the front row showed up after I came to. The rest of the theater was empty, with the exception of my dried brains and darkened blood. The two in the front row showed me their slit wrists, as they're doing right now. Is it blame in their eyes?

Over the days, months, years (has it really been that long?), more of the audience has shown up. Slit wrists, rope burns, gun shots to the head, others looking so normal I have to wonder if their guts are full of half-digested pills.

I got used to the ones who have been there night after night. The human spirit is amazing to behold, and very real. I behold it over and over again, and though I am very used to things becoming mundane, things that no mortal would ever consider as such, there are times, like when someone from that night shows up in the post brain-damage audience, that I feel true horror, regret, a sense of conscience that for all intents and purposes I should have completely separated myself from long ago.

I'm not sure what they think of me. They stare and I feel blood run down my neck, sticking the undershirt to my back like some sleek new skin. My eyes keep going back to the new girl, the pleading look on her face like I could take back time, and boy if I could . . . She looks terrified, just sitting there with the others, staring up at me like they have no choice, like I somehow damned them to this.

Perhaps I did.

I don't stand around looking into the piteous eyes of blame for too much longer. It's only because of the new girl that I stay as long as I do. Not that there is much for me on the inferno streets of Sin City.

When I leave the theater, the heat is tenfold, though it's well after ten at night. As I walk by casinos I feel gushes of sulfuric, smoky air as the doors open and close with wasted stiffs walking in and out, sometimes in perpetuity, as if they are forever forgetful of just where the hell they are going and what house they're giving their money to. It's sad, the looks of sheer listlessness in some of their eyes. What once were high pitched, happy major notes screaming from so many slot machines are now out of tune, minor and flat. It's like listening to sad music spun backwards on a record player.

The masses on the streets are no less prevalent on my return journey; in fact, there's no traffic to speak of, just a river of souls shifting through the now molten Las Vegas Boulevard, heads aflame, eyes black and dead like that of minnows. I cross over the dead souls on a bridge leading me to the Cosmopolitan, but forego walking through the casino as I did on my way to the theater. I can do without the searing heat and the psycho-jangle of the slaughter machines.

I walk around the building, passing others like myself, of whom I see in the same place every night of my goddamn . . . whatever this is. Every night of my death, my stubborn, perpetual death. I glance at a light pole, topped with what earlier had been a closed-circuit police camera which is now a bloody eye, staring as if any one of us would stray from our fate.

The elevator ride is a jerky, terrifying affair, one of those things I can never seem to get used to no matter how many nights I do this. No matter how I try, I am unable to take the stairs.

I open the door, walk into my condo, hang my hat on the coat rack, and there's no blood. Tomorrow I will begin the last day of my life. Again.

CODE BLACK

MATTHEW WEBER

WE'D HAD PROBLEMS with the Carrington family in the past, but nothing like this.

Officer Garcia and I stood next to the school principal, staring at the large circle of blood painted on the floor of the Trapper Valley High gymnasium.

"Creepy as hell," said Garcia. New to the force, he'd only dealt with shoplifters and drunk drivers. He'd been told the stories of this town, but some things a man had to see for himself. "Ain't ever seen anything like this before."

The blood formed a ring in the middle of the basketball court, and in its center lay the severed head of a deer. A nine-point buck. Scrawled along the inner edge of the circle were strange black markings and symbols I didn't recognize.

This was the school my daughter Anna attended.

"The Carrington boy did this?" I asked.

The principal pursed her lips and nodded.

"Call Klein," I told Garcia. "Tell him it's a Code Blue." That was our signal for a weird situation.

Garcia rubbed his goatee and muttered something in Spanish, then stepped away and dialed the chief.

I felt Principal Phillips' stare linger on me with a dozen unspoken questions. A stern black woman who ran the school at the point of a ruler, she expected a lot from her students as well as from everyone else. But I didn't know what these markings meant.

"Well?" Principal Phillips said.

"Looks strange," I said.

"No kidding. What's it supposed to mean? It's a threat, isn't it? It's like he marked the school, right? He's targeting us for something."

"It doesn't appear to be friendly, I'll give you that." I knelt closer to the circle and tried to make out anything legible in the markings. No such luck. Although, I did find a charred slip of paper. On it: a photo of a shoulder and a shirt collar. The face had been burned away. Judging from its size, shape and the black-and-white photography, I guessed it to be a yearbook photo snipped out of a page. "What's the kid's name again? Luke?"

"Duke. He wasn't very sly about hiding it. Some of the other students caught sight of him in here during first period when there's no PE class."

"Duke Carrington . . . " I said. "Sounds like a cowboy's name. Or a singer's."

"Doesn't look like a cowboy to me," Phillips said, extending her smartphone to me. "Here's a video."

Of course, there's a video. Kids today . . .

I watched it. The shaky picture was shot with the screen held vertically, which didn't afford a very clear view, but apparently a crowd of students confronted the guy as he etched the writings with what looked like a charred tree branch. The teenagers chided and sneered at him.

"What are you doing, freak? You fuckin' weirdo! . . . Dookie, you done gone looney like the rest of your family? . . . Take a picture! Take a picture! . . . Puke Carrington! Holy shit you're getting kicked out of school for this!"

As they approached him, the lanky, curly-haired boy in the circle hardly reacted, remaining crouched over the floor, feverishly scribing out the symbols using black ashes from a small, smoldering pile. The camera drew closer, and he finally peered up into the lens with cold hatred in his eyes—eyes encircled with the wet, red blood of the deer.

"Holy shit, motherfucker's gone crazy!" howled one of the kids, then the screen went dead.

Phillips slid the phone into her coat pocket. "One of the kids put it on YouTube."

"Wonderful . . . " This means the phone at the station will be ringing off the hook. "What happened when the video cut off? Any physical confrontation?"

"No. The other students said that's when he stood up and pulled the deer head out of a plastic bag. That's when they got scared. And they're not usually scared of him. See, the kid is from over in Shady Brake, and his family– well, they struggle financially—so some of the other students tend to give him a hard time. They're used to him shying away from *them*, not the other way around."

I'd once arrested Duke's father for public intoxication and on another occasion for beating his wife. Duke's mother was no prize herself, a total pill-zombie. But nobody deserves to be abused, and when Mr. Carrington wasn't at home to knock her around, Duke's older brother would step in on his behalf. Just a month ago, Garcia had booked 18-year-old Vince Carrington for beating up his own mom—like father, like son, I guess.

It must be hell growing up in a place like that.

"So, he was bullied," I told her, "for being poor."

Phillips sighed and looked down.

I was from Shady Brake, too, and remembered exactly what it felt like to be ridiculed for what you didn't have . . . and how angry it could make you. "But there was no fight this morning?"

She shook her head. "According to the students, he just raised the deer, stared up at the ceiling, and recited some words in another language. Then he walked out of the circle and right out of the gym without another word. No one has seen him since. We assume he left campus."

"Chief Klein's on the way," Garcia said, returning to the circle.

"Take some photos of the scene," I told him. "Get samples of the blood. Hell, I'm not sure how we're going to write this up. Vandalism? Hunting out of season? I assume the school wants to press charges?"

Phillips batted her eyelids, nervous. I could tell she didn't want to pile onto the kid's problems. Teenagers were a volatile bunch. I lived with one of my own. You didn't want to add to their angst, but you couldn't let them run wild, either. And some of them could be dangerous.

"I feel like we have to," she answered. "I mean, his actions show signs of a troubled mind. The boy needs help. And there's no other way to see this than as a threat to the other students. The safest move is to turn the matter over to the authorities. I don't want the boy back here until he's had counseling."

I thought of Anna sitting at a desk in some other room of this very campus, wearing her bookish glasses and a neat, straight ponytail. I pictured her writing in her journal, a reporter-to-be honing her craft for a bright future. Behind her, I saw a lanky kid emerge in the doorway and cast a shadow over her. He had curly hair, red eyes and carried a deer head, blood dripping from the stump of its neck. He stalked up to my daughter, and she never saw him coming.

I let out a deep breath and said, "I don't want him back here, either."

Again, I tapped on the window. Parked in the driveway of the Carringtons' trailer, Duke's mother, Mercy Carrington, sat in the front passenger seat of a Bondo-covered Ford Taurus with her head against the glass. She appeared to be asleep. I knocked a third time, when her son Vince stepped out the trailer door with two stuffed duffle bags hanging from his arms.

"Going on a trip?" I asked him.

"Can I help you?" he answered.

"Maybe. I'm looking for your brother."

He had a low-brow scowl and muscular arms that looked like they could do real damage when throwing a punch into his mother's ribs.

"He ain't here." He stepped off the stoop toward the car then hoisted the bags onto the trunk, staring at me in wait of the next question.

"Know where he's at?"

"He took off," Vince said.

"Where to?"

"Don't know."

"Why'd he run off?"

"I don't know." Vince looked down the road. "But I reckon *you* do . . ."

"You don't know *anything*?"

He threw me that scowl again. "I know things. But I don't know nothing that's gonna help *you*."

"Maybe you'd be helping your brother."

"Maybe I don't give a damn about my brother, or about helping the goddamn Trapper Valley P.D., either." He gave me a big grin like he had shit between his teeth and wanted to show it off.

"I'm sorry he did what he did," spoke a frail voice from the car. Mercy Carrington cranked down the window in front of me. "I'm sorry, officer. I told him not to mess with that stuff. Told him it was dangerous. Nobody 'round here listens to me."

Around forty-five years old, Mercy looked closer to sixty. She had stringy hair and pale, waxy skin, a hangdog face and drug-hazed eyes which always squinted, like direct sunlight might blind her. She spoke as though it took great physical effort, straining out the words with long sighs.

"What *stuff* are you talking about?" I asked her. "Your son got himself into some real trouble at school, ma'am. And we've got some questions for him down at the station. Can you tell me where he's at?"

She shook her head in a visible daze.

"He was caught vandalizing the gym," I said, as Vince slid a key into the Taurus' trunk and popped the hatch. "The Principal believes he was leaving a message—some kind of threat to the school. She's worried he means to harm the other students."

"She's worried?" Mercy said with a lilt in her voice. "Well, don't that just beat all? She's worried he's gonna hurt those other sons-of-bitches who make the poor boy's life a living hell . . . Bless her heart. Tell me, Mr. Officer. Where have you been every time he's gotten his ass kicked by the bastards in his gym class? Seems like you had plenty of opportunity since it happens every fuckin' day!"

Mercy was showing the most spunk I'd ever seen from her tired junkie ass.

"But nooooo," she said. "The only time we see your face is when one of you motherfuckers show up to throw somebody from our family in jail."

"Tell him, Mama," Vince cheered. He slammed the trunk closed, having loaded the bags.

"To answer your question, *no*," she said, "I *don't* know where he is, and if I did, I wouldn't tell you. For a minute there, I was feeling sorry for what y'all had coming to you, but I wasn't thinking straight. Y'all don't care about nobody but yourselves, and you damn sure don't care about us."

Vince opened the door and slid into the driver's seat.

"The way you're talking," I said, "it sounds like what your son wrote on that gym floor *was* a threat. What is he threatening to do?"

"No, see, you got it all wrong, Mr. Policeman." She gave me a drowsy smile. "He didn't leave a threat for you people. He left a doorway. And not a door for you . . . a door for something else."

"For what?"

Vince started the car, and Mercy cranked up the window. "Devil only knows," she said. "Devil only knows . . . that's why we're leavin'."

As the car pulled out of the gravel driveway, a crackle came from the radio in my cruiser. I walked over and reached through the window for the speaker.

"Daniels here," I said.

"Ritch, it's Klein. I'm at the high school. I need you back this way. Situation has escalated. We've got a Code Red. I repeat, we've got a Code Red."

I thought of Anna, and my mouth went dry as hay. I hit the siren and blazed a trail back toward TVHS.

Code Red meant things had gotten dangerous.

Halfway there, my mobile buzzed with a text message from Anna.

What's happening on campus? Saw the Carrington video. School on lockdown now. Nobody knows why. Not even teachers. What's the SCOOP???

I weaved the cruiser through traffic and blasted past three red lights. A school on lockdown . . . my mind raced with horrific national headlines, and I saw two stark words like blood on cotton—

Active Shooter. The damned, dreaded phrase that all too often accompanied news of a lockdown. Columbine, Sandy Hook, and now Trapper Valley, too . . . All human tragedies put into motion because some asshole kids thought it'd be fun to antagonize their awkward peers—a teenage tradition as American as apple pie. Visions of assault rifles and high-capacity magazines flashed through my head.

Please God, let it be something else.

I'd endured my own schoolyard bullies years ago, and remembered how I dreaded crossing paths with one particular shithead named Clay Quimby. That prick took great joy in my humiliation. He'd nicknamed me "trailer trash," and once even dumped a garbage can full of urine on me while I was occupying a bathroom stall. For that, I'd hated his ever-loving guts. But enough to kill him? . . . Maybe.

Klein's Bronco was parked in front of the gymnasium along with every other vehicle on the force. Two officers flanked the building's door, and others stood guard at each corner of the campus, securing the perimeter.

I screeched to a stop and ran over to Klein. "Fill me in."

I recognized his expression—those narrowed eyes and two pondering thought lines halving his brow beneath the brim of his hat. He saw scattered pieces of a puzzle but couldn't yet make out the big picture. The look was Code Red all the way.

He shook his head. "I don't rightly know what to make of it, but I got a bad feeling. Let me show you."

I followed him into the gym, nodding to Officers Garcia and Donaldson who guarded the door.

The middle of the court had been cordoned off with orange cones and plastic yellow tape. Something had happened inside the circle of blood. The hardwood and concrete in its center had ruptured upward, with broken boards and craggy chunks of subfloor piled around the edges of a crater. My first instinct told me a bomb had gone off—but that didn't quite fit.

"That look to you like something might have tunneled up out of the ground?" Klein asked as I stepped closer to the pit.

I hated to say it, but that's exactly how it looked. Roughly three feet in diameter, a nearly perfect round hole descended so deep into the earth it showed only blackness with no trace of ending, and not seeing the bottom sent a chill through my bones. "What the hell could have done that?"

Klein gazed into the blackness. "Shit. Who knows. Something straight outta hell? 'Course, that leads us to the next question."

I said it for him: "Whatever it was . . . where did it go?"

The mobile buzzed in my pocket again. Anna's number flashed on the screen.

"Where are you?" I answered.

"Dad, people are screaming!" Her voice high-pitched and breathless. "Something's happening in the hallway! People are screaming outside our room!"

"Okay, calm down. I'm at the school. Where are you? What room?"

"Mr. Harvey's class in the East Wing. Hurry, Dad!" Panicked voices shouted in the background.

"On the way!"

Klein already had his hand on his holster.

"East wing!" I said.

He shouted for backup, as I sprinted out of the gym and raced for my little girl.

As I rounded a bend in the covered sidewalk, students and teachers exploded out of the East Wing's double doors with screams and terrified faces. I scanned the crowd, searching for Anna.

"Something's in there!" someone shouted at me. "Something *big!*"

Fighting against the tide of fleeing people, I pushed through the doors to an emptying hallway.

Something lay in the floor of the corridor about fifty feet away, where the hall made a T.

I drew my sidearm as a crowd of stragglers ran past.

The thing in the floor had a twisted shape surrounded by a reddish puddle. My every muscle tensed into a knot. It did not look human. At least, not any longer.

Lord, help me keep these kids safe.

On my left, a middle-aged face pressed against the rectangular window of a classroom, shielding her eyes from glare. She saw me and put her hands together as if in prayer, mouthing a silent plea. I motioned her toward the exit behind me. Cautiously, she opened the door, looked both directions, then whispered for her students to make their escape. They slipped out of the classroom in speedy single file and dashed out of the building with their teacher behind them.

Klein caught up with me, gun drawn. "Garcia and Donaldson are covering the other entrance," he said, and then saw what was ahead of us. "What the hell is that?"

I approached the thing on the floor, and my first thought: a giant pile of puke.

It was worse. Twisted and bent, a skeletal human form lay sprawled in a pool of pink-red goo. The thing had no skin intact, but strips of clothing were mixed into the stew. An acrid stench hit me like a bag of sand, and I doubled over and spewed out my morning coffee. *Have mercy . . .* This mangled shape was likely a student. A teenager. Alive and local and brimming with potential just this very morning. And now . . . white bone shone in places through liquefied flesh.

"Anna?" I shouted down the corridor, abandoning any pretense of standard procedure. She would always come first. "Anna Daniels?!"

I tightened my grip on the Ruger. Its cold metal bit into my palm. The body on the floor looked like the victim of an acid bath, but I had an even more unsettling suspicion that maybe . . . just maybe . . . this poor soul had been partially digested.

Screams erupted from the classroom on my right. The door swung open and two girls leapt out. A third heavyset female tripped in the doorway, and more kids trampled right over her as she wailed and covered her head. I tried to reach for her, but the crowd was in a mad panic, shoving me backward. A woman—her teacher—tried to scoop her up. With Klein at my heels, I maneuvered past them both and charged inside. Then I froze before the ghastly thing hanging from the classroom ceiling.

Klein stuttered out some gibberish behind me, as two blue-jeaned legs wearing red Converse high-tops kicked wildly in mid-air. The upper half of the student's body dangled from a purplish mass bulging from the overhead air vent. I heard the kid's muffled screams and drew to fire . . . but couldn't—I'd hit the kid!

"Christ almighty!" Klein gasped at the veiny, quivering glob above us.

Those kicking legs slurped up inside some sort of orifice, and then the thing folded in on itself, and shrank back inside the vent.

"It's on the move!" I stumbled over an upturned desk and scrambled back into the hallway. The ceiling rumbled.

"Which way's it going?" Klein shouted, scanning the acoustical tiles which concealed the ductwork above us.

"Listen!"

Thumps and knocks vibrated the suspended grid. The hollow metal of the air duct moaned. With a bang, the grate of a vent ten feet away blasted off the ceiling and clanged on the linoleum floor. A purple-gray mass, fat and gelatinous, bulged out of the opening and oozed translucent slime from a hole in its center. The hole spread open and a faceless wet body slid out with a squelch and dropped to the floor in a steaming pile. It wore a pair of red Chuck Taylor high-tops, mostly dissolved but barely recognizable.

Klein and I raised our weapons and fired. We plugged the thing four or five times each, but it sucked back into the duct and disappeared again.

"Shit!" Klein shouted. He radioed Donaldson and warned them what to watch for—calling it "some kind of purple blob."

Another clamor ahead on our right. I dashed for the classroom, and my heart skipped a beat when I read the name placard: *F. Harvey.*

I threw open the door and burst inside, as the thing from the ducts slithered out of another ceiling vent. It dropped to the floor with a wet, heavy slap. Its bulbous shape, wormy but rotund like a Buick-sized maggot, pulsated within its varicose, bruise-colored skin.

The students were practically climbing the walls of the room, trying to distance themselves and make way for the exit.

"Dad!"

Anna! She cowered in the corner to my right, a book held to her chest shield-like. The terror on her face tore at me.

Klein opened fire on the creature. I did too, and we emptied both our clips, the thunder and echoes pounding my ears. Bullets plunged into the thing, but the damned beast didn't flinch, just bled black ink like it didn't matter.

But it must have had a brain, because the creature plowed ahead in the direction of the door and bulldozed eight or ten empty desks into a tangle against the entryway, sealing it off and trapping us all inside. And even half-deaf from the gunfire, I knew the screams filling the room must have shaken city hall.

The opposite wall had casement windows that would open only a few inches. One boy began bashing them with a trash can, but the shattered glass stayed in the frames.

With no better ideas, I backed up against my baby and shoved a new clip into my nine-millimeter, though I might as well have a squirt gun.

The creature reared up on one end and appeared to assess the situation. Leading with what I presumed to be its head, it slowly wormed around the room—*sniffing? searching?*—as it passed each petrified student.

As it closed in on me, my heart hammering and my finger on the trigger, I saw no eyes or nose, but the slow, methodical way it bobbed and twitched around my face suggested to me that its attacks might not be random. It was looking for someone in particular, and I prayed that Anna had never been cruel to Duke Carrington.

The creature passed by, and guilty relief flooded through me.

Along the adjacent wall, it neared a boy in a letterman jacket who had broad shoulders and big thighs. It rose up and towered above him. The other students flanking him fled to either side, as the athlete's face went white and contorted. He tried to become one with the wall behind him, clutching at the painted cinderblock. The creature loomed closer, and the kid's lips stretched to form words though no scream dared escape.

The thing drew within inches from his face. I grabbed a nearby chair in sheer desperation. Hurling it with all my strength, it bounced off the creature's back without fazing it. A circular, tooth-lined orifice opened wide in the center of its head. It spat forth a nest of writhing tongues or tentacles.

The best I could manage was: "Anna, don't watch!"

Those black tongues lashed around the boy's head like licorice whips, and he finally screamed—if only for an instant. The thing inhaled him like a hog eats a hotdog.

Anna wrapped me in her arms and buried her head between my shoulders.

Hysteria seized the students. They attacked the pile of desks that clogged the doorway, wrenching at them in a craze, or scrambling on top of them.

"Run, honey, run!" I told her.

The kids breached the entry and poured out of the classroom. She fled out the door with them. The creature appeared momentarily occupied while choking down its victim. Klein and I traded blank looks, both dumbstruck about what to do next. If we shoot it, we hit the kid inside—even though the kid was likely dead.

"We need heavy artillery," Klein said in a deadpan. He bolted out of the room.

So did I, only to find Anna waiting for me in the corridor. "I told you to get out of here!"

"I won't leave you!"

The creature suddenly squeezed through the doorway and flopped onto the hallway floor. One of its ends lifted up and swiveled in our direction.

"Damn it, run!" I hollered. "Run, Anna, run!"

With a lunge and a stretch, it bounded after us. We sprinted like hell. And, God forgive me, I fired as I ran. I lost my senses, and I pulled the trigger blindly behind me, trying to slow it so Anna could get away.

Ahead of me, she banged out of the hallway doors onto the sidewalk. The monster stayed right on my heels. "Faster! Keep going!"

She kept running down the sidewalk as I flew through the doorway behind her. The thing slowed as it pushed through the doors, but then it came barreling right after us again. The students and teachers outside scattered in every direction.

We were heading back the way I'd come, toward the gymnasium.

I had an idea: "Anna, take a left. Get off the sidewalk!"

To our right, the wall of the north wing enclosed a small courtyard, but to the left she could make a break for the baseball fields. And that's the direction she raced.

I glanced back as the thing charged at me with a burst of speed. The sidewalk veered right, so I lunged to my left in a flying leap. The thing's flank glanced my shoe as it passed. I stumbled on the landing but regained balance and ran toward Anna, who was still putting distance between herself and danger.

The creature diverted its course from us. Or rather, we'd simply been in the way. Gathering my wits, I headed back after it.

Principal Phillips saw it coming first. Standing in front of the gym's entryway with two officers, her eyes grew ten-fold and she slapped her hands over her heart. The screech she released shattered her strictly-business demeanor. The officers drew their useless sidearms and staggered backward.

"Move!" I shouted at them as I chased it. "Get out of the way!"

And they must have heard me, because they all scampered away.

The big maggot slowed in front of the gym doors and wallowed to a stop. It made a turn and squeezed through the doors back toward its point of origin.

Just then, Klein rushed up wearing a backpack-mounted tank and a handheld flame thrower—a donation to the department from the local VFW, who probably hadn't expected us to restore it to working condition.

I raised my gun mostly out of habit, and we both charged inside. Finding no sign of noise or beast, we approached the hole in the floor. In a soupy pool roughly ten feet away from it, another ruined body lay splayed across the basketball court. Shreds of the kid's letterman jacket remained barely intact—just enough for me to read the name stitched across the shoulders: *Quimby.*

I felt sick. I mean, what are the odds?

Cones and police tape lay scattered. From the slimy puddle, a broad red smear led down into the pit. The creature must have slithered back to wherever it had come from.

"Goddamn it," Klein muttered, ready to barbecue the thing.

"It's gone," I said. "Maybe it's over."

We walked closer to the hole and peered inside. No longer bottomless, the tunnel ended some six feet down, clogged with dirt and rock.

The whole ordeal defied logical explanation.

I walked outside to look for my daughter. To hug her.

But as I stepped onto the sidewalk, I felt eyes on me. A nagging suspicion. We had a visitor. I glassed the campus with a keen eye on the background scenery, looking for remote areas suited for a secret spectator. I scoured the baseball fields, the nearest parking lot, the roofs of the educational buildings. And I found him.

"There," I said, pointing.

Klein, now at my side, followed my gaze.

On a grassy hilltop alongside the bleachers of the football stadium some hundred yards away, a single lanky figure stood looking through a pair of binoculars. I knew without a doubt this was Duke Carrington, watching from a safe distance as his grand plan unleashed its carnage on everyone else. He quickly lowered the binoculars and jogged away.

I went for the car.

"Ritch, what are you doing?" Klein said from behind me.

I paid no attention, slammed the door, started the cruiser.

"Ritch, no! Wait on me!"

I was gone, the tires squealing as I swerved out of the lot and bee-lined it to the delivery route that swept up behind the stadium. That cowardly little shit had just killed at least three people, probably more. And he had to pay.

A siren wailed behind me as Klein pulled onto my tail in his Bronco. I had no plans to stop. I tore through the open gate of a chain-link fence and sped onto the blacktop that ran uphill behind the bleachers. As I reached the peak, I caught sight of Carrington scaling the fence down below. *Damn!*

I cut a sharp turn and left the road, rambling down the grassy hillside toward the fence. The car quaked and bounced, and my neck and spine rattled. With a punch of the brakes, the cruiser jerked to a stop. I popped out of the car and scaled the fence in no time, fueled by pure adrenaline.

The kid was really hoofing it, but I was a man possessed and gained on him fast. When he slowed to look back, my shoulder met his and sent him hurtling onto the ground.

"Fucking murderer!" I ripped him from the asphalt and flipped him over, straddling his torso to pin him down. He stared at me with wild, red-circled eyes as he gasped for breath. A tear hit his cheek. One of my tears. I drew back my fist to shatter his face. "You piece of shit!"

"Stop it!" shouted Klein from over my shoulder.

"This bastard just killed a bunch of kids," I said. "*Kids!*"

"He's a kid, too!"

"I don't care!" I could practically taste his blood. I tightened my knuckles.

"Don't do it, Ritch!"

I'd be screwed if I hit a minor, and this kid knew it. I saw it in his face.

"It's a Code Black!" Klein said. "Ritch . . . it's a Code Black."

I froze when he said it. Locking eyes with Duke Carrington made me want to kill him more than ever. Because I saw smugness in the kid's eyes. As I stared at him, I saw a sense of victory somewhere deep inside those red circles. The hint of a smile twitched at the corners of his mouth. Revenge was his, he thought. This little shit thought he'd gotten away with murder. After all, a monster did it, and who could possibly prove in a court of law, beyond a reasonable doubt, that this teenager was responsible for the monster?

Code Black

I unclenched my fist.

The next week, I attended three of Trapper Valley's four closed-coffin funerals. We'd found the fourth body in the boys' restroom. I did not attend the service of Greg Quimby, son of Clay Quimby, because I already had enough to bear, and I could only be so magnanimous when in bitter spirits.

Or maybe I just didn't want to see anymore.

On the following Saturday night, Officer Garcia booked Vince Carrington for a DUI, locking him in a cage next to his father, who was already being held for putting Mercy in the hospital with three fresh broken ribs.

It must be hell living in a place like that . . . But my heart grew hard, once a sympathetic fella like Duke Carrington linked arms with the devil. Cold-blooded murder crossed the line of forgiveness. That's when I quit caring about how a body turned out to be evil, and focused only on how to stop the evil. That's why I became a lawman: The pursuit of justice.

But sometimes the law does not achieve justice. Sometimes there's a loophole, like in Trapper Valley, where every once in a while, some nefarious individual exacts a kind of evil that's not covered in law books or police training, or hell, even in a science class. Some situations defied the natural order of things, and transcended the constructs of men who meant well but didn't have all the answers. In those rare situations, justice had to be carried out beyond the reach of the law, because the law just didn't have enough reach.

'Night, Dad. Love you!

The message from Anna felt like a warm breeze through the chilly evening. She always texted me goodnight when I pulled the late shift. I was sitting in my cruiser in the shadows of a parking lot alongside the darkened Trapper Valley Church of Christ, clocking speeders. But not really.

I was waiting.

Soon, I heard a rumble in the distance. I clicked the ignition over to the utility setting and quietly inched down the window. Approaching from my left, the yellow glare of headlamps lit the way for a growling diesel engine. A tinkling noise accompanied the vehicle, and I could tell from its racket and the shape of the lights that the pickup belonged to Earl Ketchum, who ran a local mechanic's shop. It was his work truck. A good bet would place pawn-shop owner Sonny Wallace in the passenger seat. They'd been deputized, so to speak, although completely off the books.

The pickup was dragging something from the back, bathed in the red glow of the taillights. A shudder ran through me when I realized Duke Carrington, wrapped in rope and gagged with duct tape, was skidding down the road tethered to a tow chain. Sparks leapt like fiery crickets as the metal links skittered over the blacktop, and beneath it all I heard the muffled squeals of the kid as the gritty asphalt sanded off his hide. At this rate, he'd be nearly skinless in a matter of minutes, just like the victims of the beast he'd summoned with that damned hill magic . . . A sentence a bit too gruesome for my taste, but I suppose it had a certain poetry to it.

It was Code Black all the way.

And I never saw a thing.

DICKEY DYKSTRA

AIRIKA SNEVE

SEE THE GUY at the far end of the office? The one prancing by the picture window on a wooden pole glued to a decapitated zebra head? That's my boss, Dickey Dykstra: the man, the myth, the legend. Owner and CEO of Chicago architectural firm Evans-Mahoney, where I work as a senior architect in a high rise owned and operated by Dykstra, Inc. Tonight, Dickey and I have a very special meeting on the books: At 6:45 p.m., we will meet in the Human Resources file room for an executive duel to the death.

Walk with me, if you don't mind a little blood.

We can always hit Target for a Tide pen later.

Bottom line: Tonight's event is almost guaranteed to include a fit of senior-level fisticuffs—at the *very* least. It may not turn out to be a 'death duel,' exactly, but I know it will come to blows. I have every intention of leaving the Incredible Galloping Dykstra in a bloody, kicked-ass sprawl on the cold filing-room floor.

We've got clients at the office today, yet Dickey—or 'Picky Dickey,' as he's fond of calling himself—is cavorting about one of those animal-headed monstrosities on which he spends so much time and money. That's right: My boss commissions and collects custom man-sized hobby horses and rides them around the office. I wish I could tell you that the zebra head on the end of Dickey's 6-foot stick wasn't real, but it is (or *was*, before the man, the myth, the legend went on safari).

You see, Dickey is a big game hunter who likes to let the world know it. He has 'a guy' who crafts the six-foot wooden poles, a guy

62

who stuffs the heads, and yet another guy who mounts the finished heads on the poles—"*You'll* fly off them poles before those heads will," he swears. I don't know when he took today's (disembodied) zebra down, but Dickey is happy to tell you whether you ask or not.

I close my eyes and try to focus on the whir of the copy machine; still, I hear the familiar scuffle of dress shoes. Half the staff is smirking, while the other half feigns focus on their monitors. You get used to pretending that this is not really happening, that Evans-Mahoney is a normal workplace, and the president of our company is not skipping around on a carcass-headed cockhorse, yelling "Yippie-ki-*yay!*"

We know the drill. This is Dickey's dog and pony show. He owns it, he runs it, and, as long as it's not blatantly illegal, he can do whatever the hell he wants.

I can smell our fearless leader's lair from here.

The office of Dickey Dykstra smells like ego, farts, and offal. Each wall is "decorated" with a hobby horse similar to the one he now straddles. Behind his desk hangs a shaggy, ginormous buffalo head mounted on a brightly burnished pole. On the opposite wall, above a bookshelf with titles like "How Patton Did It" and "Manage Like Napoleon"—which I doubt Dickey's barely skimmed—is a giraffe's head on a pole of hand-buffed pine.

I look over from the copy machine and see Dickey, flexing and glaring at

me.

I'm not intimidated. In fact, I bite back a grin.

If you hadn't noticed, Evans-Mahoney's executive nerd-herder is as much of a "card" personally as he is professionally. When someone from the company hosts a shindig at their place, Dickey is the guy sloshed, stained, and slurping straight from the faucet. Last year, at the company retreat, he spent an hour trying to burn a Forbes magazine in the fire while sermonizing about steel-cut oats: "There's no way you can be on your A-game without a daily diet of oats," swore Dickey. "No. Way."

Jane Arndt, one of our project managers, finally put the scorched Forbes out of its misery and into a plastic bag for recycling.

To be fair, Dickey does have his moments of brilliance. There's no way he could've grown the company the way he has if he was a *total* moron. Still, it's common knowledge that the guy is a buffoon and a scoundrel. You strike a deal with the Dykstra, you'd best get it in writing.

None of that fazed me, though. As the business development manager and senior designer on Dickey's A-team, I was too high up on the totem of his profit machine for him to mess with me much.

Or so I thought.

The first time he pissed me off was at last year's company Christmas party. Basically, Dickey got wasted on Jell-O shots and rubbed his doodle all over my fiancée.

I remember like it was yesterday. He slithered up nice and close behind Erin, my then-fiancée, at the pool table while she bent over for a shot. Pressing into her from behind, he gave her the old reach-around in the guise of "steadying her angles."

Yeah, *that* old song and dance.

There's my boss with his tight, tucked-in jeans and big old belt buckle, brushing his tightly-packaged womb broom against my fiancée, going, "Dynamite. Ooooh, that's just *dynamite*."

I stood at the bar in disbelief as Dickey front-frotted my woman by the light of the mini-cooler.

People were beginning to stare. My collar was getting hotter and itchier by the second, and I endured a few more minutes before strolling over to insert myself, politely asking Erin—through gritted teeth—if she'd like to order dessert.

We headed back to our table cordially enough. For me, though, the party was shot. I never said anything to Dickey, but I'm sure he could tell I was pissed.

Not that he gave a shit.

By the time Erin and I left the party in our his-and-hers evening attire, Dickey had moved on to the VP's twenty-five-year-old admin, Amber. We strolled by a furiously giggling Amber and a tipsy, tickling Dickey by the coat racks on our way out; Dickey pawed at her sides with crumbs all over his face, going, "Is that *cashmeeeere*? Dykey*likey*!"

He didn't spare us a single glance.

The ride home that night was tense, to say the least. Erin wasn't nearly as offended by Dickey's behavior as I was, but we hashed it out, and I got over it. Ultimately, the company party was but a single crack in a wall destined to crumble under far greater forces (Erin ended our engagement last April over totally non-Dickey-related issues).

While the Christmas party definitely didn't improve my professional relationship with Dickey, it didn't amount to a death duel, either.

Here's where he *really* crossed the line.

Two months ago, Dickey approved me for an all-expenses-paid client trip to Athens, Greece, and then informed me—three days before the flight—that he'd decided to take the trip himself, and I was to "stay on-base" here at the office to "keep the team on track."

"We need ya here, man," he assured. "I hate to switch this up on short notice, but we really need you. You've been the primary point of contact on the account since day one, and it's just not smart to switch horses midstream—" blah, blah, blah.

A nugget of hard Patton wisdom? Or a flimsy excuse from a guy whose plans fell through, and/or realized that a trip to Greece is far better than being stuck at the office? Either way, Dickey informed me he'd be going instead; my valued ambassadorship would best serve us here.

Was this douche canoe for real?!!

I mentioned how great my participation in the trip would be for client relations, and for offshore business development; no response. I even told him about the non-refundable deposit I'd put down to hold my first-choice resort— still, no response.

Dickey completely tuned out. He issued another half-assed apology, yawned, and said we'd reconnect at the meeting tomorrow. *Dismissed*.

Listen, I'm not always this gung-ho about twelve-hour flights to faraway corners for business, but life had been pretty flat. After Erin moved out, every day started to feel like one long, boring lunch meeting coursing toward the same exhausting train ride back to the same dark, empty apartment.

I needed a change.

Not only that, Athens would've been a (mostly) free vacation. The trip required one full workday at the client's office on Varkiza beach—*one day*— and then, for the most part, the rest of the week would've been mine for exotic dining, beach volleyball, Athens nightlife (hosted by our clients, who always knew how to party), and, who knows, maybe even a Greek goddess or two.

Of course, Dickey had to put the kibosh on it.

Still, it wasn't the stolen Mediterranean vacation which pushed me over the edge. It wasn't even the deposit I lost on the resort (that's 500 bucks I'm not getting back).

What really chapped my ass was Dickey's blatant, almost comical disregard.

Two weeks ago, our fearless leader returned from Athens suntanned, sunburnt, and smugger than ever (complete with a white Blublockers stripe across his eyes from his giant aviator sunglasses).

"The food was so good I shed a tear, Angelino," he crowed, oblivious to the dark half-moons under my eyes. "The *halvas*. The *baklava*." Then he'd slurp from his new *I Heart Greece* travel mug, which was now perma-glued to his clutch.

"Didn't even bring me a keychain, eh?" I quipped. Dickey just threw his head back and laughed like it was the funniest thing in the world.

And what was it about Greece Dickey kept grinding on about for not one, but *two* straight weeks?

It wasn't the Parthenon. It wasn't the Acropolis (which he hadn't even bothered to visit). It wasn't even the authentic Greek cuisine he feasted on day in, day out.

What really tickled his pickle was the strip clubs. From what I gathered, the food, the adventures, and the beachside resort were all just diversions from the only places Dickey gave a shit about.

The titty bars.

Neither clients nor staff were safe from his casual braggadocio. "The knocker lockers in Greece. *Man*," he reminisced, a lewd grin on his face. "We're talking not. A. Stitch. Those *European asses*." His eyes bulged. "*Dynamite*."

Until Monday, all I could do was nod. The level of Dickey's buffoonery legitimately blew my mind. Two weeks of lascivious, stentorian babble about a vacation he'd casually plucked from my hands—on egregiously short notice, no less—and he didn't even have the courtesy to show me an ounce of respect.

After that, everything he did pissed me off. His hoss-riding shoe scuffles were like nails on a chalkboard, and I was seconds away from a meltdown when a game-changing email crossed my desk.

Like a bolt out of the clear, Greek sky.

On Monday, Dickey accidentally included me and a couple of others in an email about an under-the-table design deal with Stedmark, Inc.—a subsidiary of a company called Abramowitz-Martin, which was a direct competitor of a firm (with which) we were about to close a multimillion-dollar investment deal.

Thing was, the investors required a non-compete clause in their contract; thus, we'd already agreed not to work for their competitors, and that we'd disclose such if we did. Though Stedmark wasn't directly named as a competitor, its execs were shareholders from Abramowitz-Martin—a company which *was* specifically named.

I knew our investors would be pissed if they found out . . . and, what do you know, we were set to close the deal in less than two hours.

I thought about Dickey's crotch couched up to my ex at the pool table. I thought about ticklin' Dickey and the VP's admin by the coat racks, Dickey exclaiming "Dickey*likey*! Mmmm, Dickey*likey*!" as he (inappropriately) pawed at her sides.

Dickey, with that shit-eating, I-can't-help-it grin: *The moussaka, Angelino! It was so good I cried!*

Those asses . . . dynamite!

Booya!!!

Back in the conference room, while Dickey laughed with other higher-ups about the corpse carts in India, I leaned back and smiled.

Less than two hours until the big investor meeting, and I hadn't been that excited about work in years.

Yippie-ki-yay.

Name's Dickey. Dickey Dykstra. Chief Executive Officer of the firm set to take over the build and design space from Chicago to Peru. The numbers are coming in strong, baby. We've got something special here, something dynamic.

But hey, I could talk shop all day. Let's get down to business.

See that little Guido over there mean-mugging me by the copy machine? That's the lead engineer and business dev, Michael

Angelino. Let's just say I'm about to mentor him in the space of ass-blasting into kingdom come. We just lost out on a two-million-dollar business deal, and why?

Michael Angelino.

I had everything lined up. We were talking to this company—legally, I can't give you their name, but think big. We're talking $100,000,000 last year *alone*. You've seen the name, you've shopped it, you'd know it if you heard it.

OK, it's Buttafuoco. Buttafuoco Home Goods.

Yeah, THAT Buttafuoco.

So Buttafuoco was set to pull the trigger on a two million-dollar investment deal until Angelino fucked it up. Their CEO—some butch in a suit—had the pen in her hand, and everything.

Angelino was just *thrilled* to run and grab the contract off the printer. He comes back with the documents, which *just so happen* to include a printout of an email about the business deal I'd *specifically* asked the recipients to disregard (Stedmark, if you must know!)

Yeah, OOPS.

The Buttafuoco butch was all, "What's this?!" and then they all swarm over for a look. Angelino claimed he must've hit the wrong button in all the excitement and missed the extra printout.

My ass.

Needless to say, Buttafuoco was not happy. I tried to reason with them, tried to explain how minor the Stedmark deal actually was, but they were having none of it. I looked Angelino in the eye right then, and I swear the punk was smiling.

Buttafuoco said they'd get back to us, but that was two days ago. They haven't taken a single one of my calls since.

Two million smackeroos!

That son of a bitch. Whose team is this joker on, anyway?!

Technically, I knew I couldn't fire Angelino for the Buttafuoco thing. According to my lawyer, there was no way to prove it was anything but a mistake—but I knew the truth.

"Dick," I says to myself, "You're gonna have to get creative." So I set up a spreadsheet with all kinds of ways to yank Mikey's chain. You don't make a fool out of a general on his home field—especially not THIS general.

I'm not usually one to shit where I eat, but in Angelino's case, I decided to make an exception.

Booya.

Buttafuoco left the meeting without even shaking Dickey's hand. The two million-dollar bridge had not only been burnt, it was incinerated.

As soon as the door closed, Dickey unleashed a *"Fuuuuuuck!"* so loud and strangled, even the second floor heard.

Sweet, sweet satisfaction.

I hit the john after the Buttafuoco fiasco for my usual morning pinch. There I am, parked on the shitter with the newest C-Level (magazine) on my lap, and I'm so steamed I can't crap. Literally, I've got *steam* coming out of my *ears*, but there is *nothing* coming out of my ass.

Two million bucks!!!

I was even more fired up on the drive home. There I was, fuming in my 4x4 with *Now That's What I Call Music* on blast, and Paula Cole comes on the deck.

I cranked it to 11 and played it on loop. By the time I pulled into my driveway, I was screaming at the top of my lungs: "WHAT WILL IT BE, ANGELINO? WHAT WILL IT BE???"

I stormed out back, shoved my big gas grill over, and ripped plants out of the garden while screaming the lyrics over and over. Lights came on, and the neighbors' dogs started barking.

I didn't care. If they had a problem, they can suck my manscaped *cajones*!

After a shave and a fine brown shit (none of that weak, rabbit-turd, no-fiber bullshit I see floating in the office bowl!) I studied my reflection long and hard.

I knew what I needed to do.

I went into my home office, grabbed a box of business cards, and contemplated the words that would put this dandy little conflict in motion.

Yee-haw.

"Where: #101 (Basement level / Secure entrance). When: 6:45 p.m. Who: D. Dykstra & M. Angelino. What: A confidential meeting."

This was the invite, written in pen on the back of a scribbled-out business card, Dickey handed me at the office cafeteria yesterday.

I was standing in line at the register when I felt a hard tap on the shoulder. I turned around, and it's Dickstra. He hands me this business card and says, *"Be there."*

I read the card. At first, I'm confused, but the look on Dickey's face told me everything I needed to know. With a stone-cold glare of my own, I assured him I'd be there.

Listen. Dykstra may have a couple of inches on me (I'm 5'6", he's about 5'9"), and he may lift more than I do, but I think he'd be surprised at what a smaller guy like me can do. I grew up in Boston. I've been in my share of scraps.

Less than four hours until I plant my boot in the seat of Dickey's designer men's jeans.

Booya! Whattaya know, it's greasy Angelino in the elevator across from me. My elevators are glass, so I have a crystal-clear view of that punk standing in front, giving me the stink eye.

It's 6:30—only fifteen more minutes until Project Takedown kicks off, and I'm on my way to the file room for some pre-game prep.

I've got a little something extra for Mikey, and I wouldn't want him to spoil the surprise. I'll tell you *one* thing you can take to the bank:

Dickey don't lose.

Holy shit, Dykstra's in the elevator across from me. We're going down at exactly the same speed. You couldn't have timed this better if you tried.

He's probably headed for the basement, but I plan to stop on the main floor for a change of clothes and a Coke. Honestly, I haven't been in a fight since high school. I've got to get my head in the game.

Dickey flexes and glares at me as the elevators drop, and I make no secret of my laughter.

Even from here, I can see Dykstra's face heat to a dusky brick red.

Picky Dickey here, dispatching from Room 101.

Five minutes to 6:45. The party's in full swing, and we're all geared up.

Don't be late.

My elevator alights on the ground floor. There's no one at the information desk, and there doesn't appear to be a single other human soul around. I've never seen the place so dead. It's like the entire staff has been dismissed—and for all I know, they have.

This is Dickey's building. *He's* the cock of *this* walk.

I head to the vending machine and silent hallways unroll before me like after-hours back alleys. I jump when my Coke clatters into the vending tray. I can't lie, I'm a little nervous now that things are down to the wire—but not nervous enough to back down.

There's no way I'm giving Dickey the satisfaction. Hell, he's smug enough already.

Only ten more minutes until the duel.

Ivanhoe's away.

It is now 6:45, and I am standing in the doorway of #101.

Dickey's got the lights off in there. I'm not chickening out, by any means, but I'm also not strolling into a pitch-dark room with an agitated executive nearby.

Finding the room was easy enough. The basement was empty and unlocked, as Dickey had said it would be, and all I had to do was follow the clearly-marked signs around the building to #101, easy peasy.

Now, I peer inside to scope the layout. From what I can tell, #101 is a spacious, high-ceilinged brick room lit only by a single, dangling bare bulb at the far back. The bulb throws a low spotlight over a gym mat with a pair of bleachers on both sides, like a high school wrestling match.

How very, very Dickey.

There are boxes of what appear to be ancient office receipts, printers, and sheet-covered office equipment gathering dust on shelves and worktables. Aside from the gym mat at the back—which is a long, dim walk down the middle of a dark cement basement away, might I add—the place looks like a cross between a workshop and a storage space.

The man, the myth, the legend emerges from the shadows and steps out onto the mat.

And I try not to laugh.

Dickey flexes and glares before me in all his buttoned-up, business casual glory. Even from here, I can see he's still wearing his Bulgari watch, and his shirt is neatly tucked in for the brawl.

What a pro.

I sneer at the boxes overflowing around him. "So much paper, Dickey. I'm disappointed in you." It just flys out. "I thought you'd be completely digital by now."

His smile falters, but he doesn't lose his cool.

"Are you game?" he asks.

I'm sure as shit not backing out now, so I reply, "You know it."

I cross the threshold into #101.

"Welcome to my workshop," calls Dickey. His arms are folded in full smug- mode. My blood's already boiling as I walk to the mat. Dickey points a slim, credit card-sized remote at the door, and it closes with a startling clang.

"I'll get the lights," he says, and jogs over to flick a bank of switches on the wall. Cold fluorescent lighting floods the room, and I see what's there.

What's been there all along.

In the vaulted brick basement, strung up on wire from floor to ceiling, is a virtual museum of the oversized wooden pezdispensers Dickey calls 'cockhorses'—but, unlike the ones in his office, these aren't all animals.

Many of these are human.

My horrified eyes sweep over the human-headed hobby horrors galloping amongst the elk, zebras, gibbons, and antelope. Some are men, and some are women. Some sport neat professional haircuts, while others have hair like disheveled beaver pelts. Some are adorned by business ties and costume jewelry, while stirrups dangle from the handles of others.

Most horrific of all are the hordes of severed human heads propped up on the bleacher seats like spectators at a baseball game. They stare vacuously at me, into me, and through me, impassively awaiting the match.

Heads. Heads everywhere, staring into space.

Dickey flashes his true grin, a shark's grin. The one he gets when he closes a deal or shoots an animal—or, as it turns out, a person.

I feel like I'm going to pass out, piss my pants, or both. A mechanical stuffed fish shoots out of the wall like a boxing glove on a spring, and I leap away, screaming. Dickey laughs, his eyes twinkling merrily.

He's loving every second.

"*Fuck this shit!*" I scream, and make a break for the door. Dickey stands with his arms folded, calmly watching me yank the handle—which is as locked as I knew it would be.

Shit.

I'm backed against the door like a mouse under a flashlight beam.

"*Why*?" I gasp, desperately casting about for something, anything I can use as a weapon.

"Just born to hunt, I guess." Dickey yanks a sheet off a shrouded rectangular shape, revealing a row of human cockhorses displayed neatly on a rack. He nods like the proud owner of a priceless guitar collection. "Go ahead. Pick a horse," he says, and snatches one. "I call this one *Nashville!*"

My heart slams like a one-man mosh pit. My knees threaten to buckle. I bite down on the tip of my tongue, and bright, coppery pain clears my vision and brings me back to life.

I don't have the luxury of passing out. I know exactly what Dickey's got in store for me if I do.

"Who *are* all these people?" I ask, reeling.

"People?" Dickey shrugs. "Accountants. Consultants. Some architects, what have you, quite a few vagrants . . . I even have some C-levels!" His eyes light up, and he stamps the floor with his chosen stallion (i.e. the head of a sandy-blond man with a neat Republican haircut).

He passes it back and forth between his hands like a football. "Nashville, *woohoo!*"

"So this is what the meeting was really about?" I ask. "My head on a pole?"

Dickey claps and barks a hollow salesman's laugh. "Oh, come on. Those are *so* last year." He yanks a sheet away from a tall, shrouded shape I hadn't noticed. "You get to be my first *Segway!*"

With a flourish, Dickey reveals the two-wheeled contraption for which he's planning to sever my spinal cord.

It's a Segway, all right, and it's waiting for my head like a morbid crown jewel. I can tell from the domed metal bars atop a spinal steering post, that this thing was specifically engineered to sport a human head.

I take in the black pneumatic tires and ergonomic handlebars designed to jet Dickey across this hand-hewn house of horrors at a brisk 12.5 miles an hour.

"I'm expanding," Dickey says, and takes a step toward me. "Now pick a horse."

I simply answer, "No."

"You're scared."

I shake my head, and his eyes darken.

"Who, me?" My voice comes out steady and strong. My fists tighten. "Afraid of Picky Dickey and his incredible investment plan?"

"YOU!" Dickey roars and jabs a finger at me. He lets out a "HYAH!" like a cowboy spurring on a steed.

And then he charges me.

What happens next is more of an awkward scuffle, and less like the *Total Recall* fight scene of my daydreams. Dykstra is half past forty, after all, and I'm no spring chicken at 37.

I wrench Dickey's man-horse out of his hand right away. Its scratchy man-hair brushes my wrist on its way to the floor, where it thuds harmlessly out of reach. The fight turns into a clumsy wrestling match—but, to Dykstra's credit, it seems all that knuckle-headed weightlifting of his has done him good. He's in decent shape . . . better shape than I am, anyhow.

We pull a plastic shelf over us in the scuffle. Dusty office supplies clatter to the floor. I glimpse Dickey's precious *I Heart Greece* travel mug hitting the mat, but it doesn't break. Dickstra's got paper clips in his hair, and I can't help but laugh crazily.

Soon, however, Dickey has me in a sleeper hold I can't clobber my way out of. He's yelling, *"Should've eaten your steel-cuts, motherfucker!"* as he tightens his hold.

I knew I shouldn't have cancelled that gym subscription.

Damn you, Dickey. Damn you and the hobby horse you rode in on.

That's when I see the mug and reach out for it with a shaking hand . . .

I clobber the Incredible Galloping Dykstra with his own *I Heart Greece* travel mug.

Its convenient porcelain handle makes it delightfully easy to slam into the skull of the smarmiest business owner/undercover serial killer this side of Chicago.

KAPOW.

Dickey goes down like a sack of laundered goods.

The whole thing is bloody. It's chaotic.

It's fucking golden.

Thanks to me, the Windy City Whacker (you heard it here first), now lies in a bloody, kicked-ass heap on the cold filing room floor. I don't think he's dead— his chest is still rising and falling, despite all the blood—but he'll definitely be out for awhile.

I fumble Dickey's keycard from his pocket, swipe it, and heave my sweat-soaked, blood-spattered body through the doorway and into the hall. From there, I collapse and simply lie on the floor, panting.

I'll call for help in a sec. Right now, my whole body feels like it's been flattened by a Buick. I'd love to whale on Dickey with one of his own creations, but I'm not going near that room.

So what happens now?

A media circus, I'm sure. Maybe a nationwide police investigation. God knows who or what else will turn up in Dickey's house of horrors, but I'm sure it'll all come out soon.

After that?

Your guess is as good as mine. All I know is that, after this shit show, I am in desperate need of a vacation.

Athens, here I come.

23 To 46

Paul Stansfield

WHEN HE LOOKED back on it, Matthew Buchinger realized that the first time that they had actually spoken to him was that time in June. He'd been enjoying some weed, watching TV. Watching being the operative word, since he couldn't honestly admit to following any program while high; the next day he wouldn't recall any significant details about the shows he'd viewed. The voice was commanding and seemed to originate from inside of him. It said, simply, "Stop smoking. You're hurting us."

In his condition, Matt had found this very humorous. He'd brayed some thick laughs and taken another hit. What a trip! His laughter died, though, when the voice spoke again, even more forcefully this time. So forcefully, it had made his head ache. "We said stop it. Don't make us hurt you."

That had done it. Matt had put out his bowl and thrown it against the wall. Then he'd commenced with a search of his apartment. Checked that all his doors and windows were locked. Checked the damp towels underneath the doors (a silly precaution, now, but Matt was nothing if not paranoid). Then he looked for hidden cameras by lifting each mirror off the wall and examining the backs, and by peering intently at every light fixture. Finally, fear overtook him. Terrified, yet ashamed at the same time, he'd pulled off his blanket, wrapped himself in it, and had cowered beneath his bed.

He made it a week before the voice returned. He was home alone, this time watching a standup comedian on cable. Sober. The incident of last week had scared him off the pot for the present time.

"Hello, Matt. We're your sperm. We'd like to talk to you." Matt was preparing to repeat his frenzied search of his apartment when the voice continued. "No, don't bother to search for hidden mics or cameras. We're within you, part of you. Relax."

Hesitantly, he spoke up. "My sperm? How are you able to communicate with me? I must be going nuts."

"No you're not. Your mental state is normal. Some neuroses and such, but well within average limits. And by the way, don't speak out loud. Just think your answers and questions. We don't know how this has happened, but over the past few months we've become conscious and have learned how to communicate with you."

Matt laughed nervously. "Yeah right. I'm having weird flashbacks from those 'shrooms. I need a drink." He started to get up.

Suddenly the voice filled his head, impossibly loud, piercing. "No! We're real, and we are talking to you. Your sperm, yes! Now sit down and pay attention."

Feeling strange and confused, Matt did as he was told. The voice continued, this time in a moderate tone. "Now that we've established who we are, let's talk about what we want. And that is, fertilization. You're twenty-eight and haven't fathered any children! That's a disgrace. You're going to fix that."

"Disgrace? I've never been married or even been in a long-term relationship. It's no accident that I don't have kids. I haven't been ready yet. So I'm careful."

"Ready? Careful? Married?" The voice was snide and slightly louder. "None of these things matter. What matters is you've got millions of sperm, all waiting for a chance to become human, and you prefer to kill them in a poison-filled sheath of latex, or in a toilet, or through inactivity! But *you* have your principles! Whoopee fuckin' do! Is that supposed to comfort us when we die, uselessly?"

"There's life after conception, you know. Life that can be filled with problems if certain needs aren't met. Practical, physical, and emotional. Needs I'm not capable of fulfilling right now."

"Well never mind all that," the sperm said coldly, "Clearly we're not going to convince you. The important thing is, we run this show. Do as we say or we'll drive you mad. Perhaps it'll ease your precious conscience when you realize you have no choice."

Matt's thoughts mimicked the sperm's iciness. "You run the show? Oh really. Tell me, who am I going to impregnate if I'm locked in a straightjacket in a padded room? Or dead with a brain aneurysm? You sperm don't need me, huh?"

There was a long moment of silence while the sperm thought this over. "Look, okay. We've gotten off track. We got excited and resorted to childish threats. Yes, we do need you. Both of us wear the pants in this relationship. Remember, we're on the same team here. We only want to spread our genes, live forever. Something you benefit from as well. But we'll take some time off, let everyone get calm again. We'll talk to you tomorrow night."

"You were thinking of sex," the sperm said, "Very good. Keep that up and we'll all be happy."

Matt sighed. He'd been thinking of a woman in his office. Imagining throwing her down on the conference table during some dull meeting and having at it right there, in front of all his coworkers. But the little buggers had sucked all the fun out of this fantasy. "Yeah, yeah. Who am I speaking to? Which sperm, I mean? Are you the leader?"

"I'm not an individual. I'm a collective voice of all your sperm. We are all separate, yes, but also joined together as a whole, for a common goal. We individuals are constantly dying and being created, of course. But all with a mind toward our single purpose."

"I see. How communistic. Even if you're not an individual, I think I'll call you Lenin."

"Call us what you will, although we're only interested in economic and class matters so far as they affect you fathering children."

"That's another thing. You're sperm. How do you know about communism, or about any non-reproductive stuff, anyway?"

"We have access to your mind. What you know, we can know. Although we focus on procreative thoughts, usually, as you probably expect."

"So how come my other cells don't talk to me?"

"Not sure. They are aware, and can think. We can read them. Terribly boring. Your stomach cells, for example, only think about the best way to digest each piece of crap you throw into it, what percentage of this chemical and that chemical, etc. And it's paranoid about digesting itself in its own juices. Snore."

"Yeah, don't you just hate cells who are obsessed with their own boring agenda, to the exclusion of everything else?"

"Shut up. Excuse us for caring about your future, slacker."

"That doesn't really answer my question, though. Why don't my stomach cells badger me about eating better foods or something like that? Why suffer in silence?"

"We don't know, and don't care. Fuck your stomach! It does its job and that's all that matters." A pause. "Perhaps . . . We think it's because they're full cells. That's the only difference we can come up with."

"Full cells?"

"Full. Forty-six chromosomes. We have twenty-three, of course. So we join with the twenty-three chromosomed eggs to make a full forty-six zygote. But enough background. What are your reproductive plans? And before you get testy, we've come up with a new plan. We won't drive you insane, you were right, that would be counterproductive for everyone, but we can annoy the crap out of you. Say bombard your mind with loud chatter when you're trying to work or talk with someone. But why focus on ugliness? We're sure you'll cooperate."

"Yeah, I will. But you have to compromise, too. You have to recognize practical limitations."

"Fair enough. Such as?"

"I can't just go around having sex with every woman I meet. There's nasty diseases, for one. Diseases that can kill me. And there's legal matters, too. If I have several bastards, I have to pay child support. If I don't, or can't pay, I can be sent to jail. And in jail I certainly can't impregnate some guy's ass."

"True, okay. How about if you traveled to poor Catholic countries a lot and impregnated virgins? Less chance of disease, more likely that they'll have the child."

"If they're poor Catholic virgins, they'll probably be less likely to have sex with anyone, much less a foreigner."

"If they won't, then rape them and never return to that particular country."

"No way! I'm a scumbag, I'm willing to knock someone up and leave if the alternative is constant harassment from you, but I'll never, repeat, never, rape someone. I don't care what you do. And if you harass me too much, I'll kill myself, and you with me. You can't prevent split second actions, like turning the car into oncoming traffic."

"Okay, okay . . . We're just brainstorming, that's all. We'll come up with something else."

It was silent for several minutes, then Matt spoke up happily. "I got it! Sperm banks! A great compromise! Both partners happy. You get fertilized and I don't have to abandon my ethics. It's all voluntary and safe."

"It's better than nothing . . . " the sperm sounded more guarded. "But how can we be sure they'll pick you often enough?"

"I should do well. I'm healthy, no bad genetic predispositions that I'm aware of. Fairly intelligent, successful, good looking, too. And you can do your part. Step up the production, make sure my sperm count is high, and I'll be more tempting."

"Okay, that'll work," the sperm replied. They spent the next few minutes explaining what he would have to do to ensure high sperm count, such as switch to boxers and various dietary hints. Then they fell silent for the night.

The pre-come was really dripping now. Matt was close. With his left hand, Matt kept pumping, while his right picked up the vial and positioned it near his penis. A minute later he ejaculated smoothly into the container, not missing a single drop. Ahh. His toes uncurled, and a second later he was all business. Matt placed the now filled vial securely on the counter. Next, he washed thoroughly, removing the oily residue of the Vaseline. Then a quick check to make sure he hadn't spilled any on the chair or rug (clean), a few blasts of Lysol around the room, and he was finished. He rolled up his porn mag, stuffed it in his inner coat pocket, and strolled out.

The nurse looked up blandly as Matt walked up to her counter. He handed her the vial, which she took with a gloved hand. She then made a few marks on some papers, smiled slightly, and said, "Thank you Mr. Buchinger. Your check will be processed tomorrow. You should get it by Friday."

Matt muttered a quick "Thanks" and walked out of the clinic. As always, he nearly sprinted down the hall, looking around furtively to see if anyone had seen which office he'd come out of. No one else in the hall, though, thank goodness. He relaxed some and went out to his car.

The shit he put up with to placate the little fuckers! Matt had been donating for three months now, and it wasn't getting much easier. He'd figured it'd be a piece of cake, but he hadn't thought it through. Hadn't figured on how humiliating it was to admit to masturbation. That's what the sperm donation basically was, multiple relivings of his teenaged nightmare of being caught jerking off. Only now he was an adult, so he didn't even have the raging hormone excuse. It was ridiculous. He knew everybody, or at least 99% of people masterbated, he'd made hundreds of jokes about it to his friends over the years, but still, when you actually went into a room by yourself and then came out later, and handed someone your load, it still brought embarrassment somehow. The employees were professional and low key, but it didn't stop him from feeling like he was fourteen again, and his stepdad was banging on the door, saying other people wanted to use the bathroom too.

Sigh. In some ways it was getting better, he guessed. The second time he'd been there he'd misjudged and missed the vial. Had spooged all over his clothes and the rug. That had been about the lowest time. He'd furiously cleaned up the mess with wet paper towels and sprayed almost a pint of Lysol all over the rug. As he did, he'd tried hard not to think about how many other guys had done the same thing. Ugh. Later he'd poured a ton of detergent on the day's clothes to try to sterilize them, feeling like Lady Macbeth, only instead of blood it was semen stains. And then had come the realization that he had no sample. Matt had panicked and walked out, avoiding the nurse entirely. Luckily, they were undoubtedly taught not to challenge the depositors, so he'd escaped without further ado. That was another thing. He had a pet theory that the sperm bank only hired unattractive, elderly nurses. Not a one of the female employees was under sixty, it looked. He theorized that this was to cut down on guys hitting on them, suggesting other ways to obtain the sperm sample.

A horn punctured his thinking, and Matt accelerated under the now green light. Ever since his sperm had started talking to him, he'd been continually distracted and jumpy. Not to mention frustrated. The bank only permitted two deposits a week, at least three days apart. Any sooner and the sperm count would be lower. And, alas, this was his only allowable sexual outlet. The sperm wouldn't let him jerk off normally and dumping your load in a medical cubicle twenty miles from home during set business hours took the spontaneity away, and most of the fun.

As for sex, forget it. They absolutely wouldn't let him do it with a woman unless he didn't use protection, and the woman was fertile and pro-life. Obviously, finding a woman with all these qualifications—and disease free—had proven to be futile, at least so far. Furthermore, Matt still didn't want the emotional and financial responsibility of a kid, anyway. So there were a lot of blue ball enhanced days. They even ruled his dreams; whenever Matt was having a sex dream the sperm would wake him up before he turned it into a wet one.

It was affecting his social life significantly. His frustration (and fear of his sperm) made him edgy and nervous. His friends and family had already expressed concern, for which his explanations seemed insufficient. As for interacting with women, that was forbidden, unless she met the former criteria.

If Matt innocently flirted with a woman, he'd hear the looming familiar voice say, "This is not productive. She's not willing to have any kids with you right now, is she? Cut it out, or you know what'll happen." They were perfectly willing to remind him, too, if he forgot how intensely painful they could be. Matthew Buchinger had gone from a fairly popular, happy-go-lucky, moderate ladies man to a withdrawn, lonely, sort of guy.

But, on the plus side, the sperm were keeping up their end of the bargain if Matt kept up his. As long as he followed their directives they left him virtually alone. Not completely, of course, because he knew they were still there, monitoring him constantly, but it was an improvement.

They'd actually been rather cheerful and supportive of late, once they (and Matt) had learned that three women were pregnant with his sperm (a kindly nurse had told Matt this much, no more, and this tidbit was more than enough. The sperm couldn't have cared less who the mother was, as long as she had their child. "Finally, your life has meaning," they'd said, "Good job!"

As Matt entered his apartment, he saw his answering machine message light was blinking. He hit the play button. "Hello, this is MCI with an offer," snap, he fast forwarded through the unwanted sales pitch. Then, a breathy voice spoke: "Hey baby, it's Gladys. I know it's been a while. Just wanted to know how you're doing, and maybe get together for a drink. Call me, 590-8632, if you forgot."

Matt grinned. Gladys. Or "Glad-Ass," as he liked to call her. She did have a great ass. Round and firm. He replayed the message to double check the number, and then wrote it down. He'd just started to dial when a slightly piercing mind shriek went through him, causing him to hang up.

"Now, now," the voice scolded. "Remember: no plans for immediate kids, no relationship. We know she's not the one. Don't encourage her."

"You want me to lie?"

"We want you to give full life to us, something you seem unwilling to do. So, yes, if it keeps you from wasting us, and precious time, then lie. Or tell the truth and have her think you're insane. Either way."

Matt petulantly refused to call back at all. Instead he moodily plopped down on his couch and clicked on his TV, flipping through 63 channels almost without pause. He did stop on a commercial featuring Lauren Hutton though. Still easy on the eyes, he mused.

"That's your problem," the sperm boomed. "How stupid are you? She's clearly past menopause. Her usefulness is done. Your taste in women is appalling. Like that actress you were gawking at yesterday. The skinny one. Not even enough body fat to conceive! You'd send us into that barren hole?!"

Matt ignored them. He was too tired of fights of this sort. Encouraging them just led to more headaches. Five minutes passed, and he tried to get into a cop show. Two detectives were smacking around a guy to force a confession. Then, a beer commercial came on, followed by a sanitary pad one.

That set them off again.

"The gall of these women," they raged. "All proud to be comfortable during their periods. What a crock! They should be in pain. They need the reminder that they're failures! Every period is the death of an egg! And there's only about 400 of them! That's even worse than you males wasting millions of us! They should call them Death Pads, and make every woman who wasted an egg that month wear one stuck to her head, as a badge of shame!"

Even though he knew the consequence, Matt lost his temper. "You little shits! Once again, you're showing your ignorance. People aren't baby-making machines! If they did as you said and every woman used every egg, every guy didn't waste a single load, we'd be overrun with people! And then most of them would die from lack of food and necessities. More death for you! What do you say to that, huh?"

"That's full-people business. You work out all of that." This only further enraged Matt. He thought vicious curses at his sperm, belittling them, damning them. They didn't respond to subsequent challenges. That was typical of them. Whenever he brought up their hypocrisy, they pleaded ignorance, saying poor "half people"—as they also referred to themselves—didn't know enough about the big world, they only focused on themselves. Not that it stopped them from giving their opinions when they did think they had the answer. They simply refused to see the big picture, or didn't care.

Matt's mental ranting finally dwindled. He paused, then thought calmly, "Why are you talking to me, anyway? Bothering me with your stupid opinions. I was a good boy, remember? Gave—"and here he did a poor imitation of Carl Sagan "—Billions and billions of your boys a good home in a vial."

"Don't break your arm patting yourself on the back. You do the bare minimum, no more. Three pregnancies and you think that you're Mr. Father of the Year. You need the reminders to keep yourself in circulation."

"Well, actually, three kids are probably more than the average guy my age, so I think I'm doing pretty good."

"Oh bullshit. So just because you're just above all those wrong people, that makes you right? No, you're all still wrong. You're just less wrong than most. But, more to the point, we're naturally more concerned with you than others. Pass yourself on. Live forever. It's like a game. The person with the most kids wins, has the most chance of eternal life. You remember that doctor who worked at a fertility clinic, who was punished for impregnating seventy women with his sperm and not the ones they picked out? He should be your hero."

Matt was already tired of the argument. It was always so pointless. He was never going to convince them, or they him. So, to interrupt their ranting he changed the subject.

"Hey, isn't there a lot of competition amongst you sperm? As to which one gets to fertilize the egg? You guys must have major brawls over that."

"Of course not. We're all part of the same group. It doesn't matter which individual fertilizes the egg, as long as one of us does. We just swim, and whoever gets there first is it."

Matt didn't respond to this, and he was relieved that the sperm didn't elaborate. He flipped through some more channels but didn't find anything of interest. Oh well. Might as well start a new book. He thought the newest Heller book was in his bedroom.

As he walked to his room, his eyes happened to land on the answering machine again. Once again, his mind went back to days with Gladys. A real hottie. He still remembered how good she was at giving head. Did that trick with her tongue—

"Enough reminiscing. Particularly of that behavior. Oh, real nice for you. Useless death for us! That kind of stuff is worse than whacking off, even! Because it's a tease. Right kind of partner, wrong hole. It's like—"

"All right, shut the fuck up! You monitor every activity and force me to abandon the ones you disapprove of. Now I can't even think my own thoughts? Are any of you wasted when I think about recreational, non-reproductive sex? Now you have to control everything? Let me have some fun. No one is getting hurt by this!"

The sperm went quiet at this. They didn't resume conversation, or make any more snide comments. Matt sighed in mild triumph and went into his room. He intentionally thought some more about "useless death" sex, more out of spite rather than a pleasant recalling. Then he picked up the Heller book and spent the next hour or so immersed.

Finally, though, his eyes got heavy, and he started having to reread passages. Time for sleep. Matt got up and brushed his teeth. Then he switched off his light and got under the covers. After a few minutes he decided to needle his sperm some more; he was still pissed.

"Goodnight, half-men. Guess you agree with Spock in Star Trek III, when he mentioned, 'The needs of the many outweigh the needs of the few or the one.'"

The sperm answered softly and carefully, obviously not wanting another frenzied rebuke. "But we're not the many. We—as well as the rest of all your cells—are part of you, the one. So actually, the opposite is true. The needs of the one—all of us, and you, combined—outweigh the needs of the other people."

The next few months were Hellish. The treaty between Matt and his sperm barely held. Tensions ran high. Every time Matt started to relax even a little bit, they'd be there to criticize him for not fertilizing enough women. They'd also learned a new, nasty trick. In addition to the headaches they started to give him frequent blue balls, as a painful type of manipulative encouragement.

Running out of ideas, he'd begun reading up on healthy living habits, assuring the sperm the research was simply to enhance his physical health in order to attract better breeding mates, of course. They'd been suspicious but seemed pleased. The exercise and meditation he started engaging in gave Matt the mental strength to subdue the sperm's constant intrusions. Just enough to make life more tolerable. He was still constantly nervous, never sure what they'd do or say, but the meditation made things a bit better.

Matt enjoyed the new-found peace for another three weeks. But the final straw came when his neighbor Harvey held a house party. It had been Matt's first socializing in months. Aided by beer and shots, Matt was able to relax and found himself being hit on by Harvey's housemate Miranda. Back in her room they started fooling around. Miranda seemed pretty drunk, but so was he. Then she puked, down the side of her bed and looked ready to pass out.

Matt pulled back and stood up. He wasn't a rapist. At that point the sperm had protested. Issues of consent didn't matter to them. Only fertilization.

In that moment, Matt learned that like himself, the sperm had gotten stronger too. What happened next was like an out-of-body experience. Against his will, his body returned to the bed. Then he was atop Miranda, grabbing at her clothes. His mouth opened, and he heard them using his voice to speak.

"Enough of your ridiculous moralizing! Impregnate this bitch RIGHT NOW!"

Here Matt counter-punched, using the mind tricks he'd been learning and practicing, under the guise of health research. But even so, he was barely able to get away from Miranda and the party. Finally back at home a pint of vodka successfully sedated all of them for the night.

The next morning, Matt was on the move as soon as he awakened. It was time to enact the plan, he'd been researching. The hangover seemed to dull the sperm somewhat. He managed to think only about pregnancy trivia during the ride to the surgeon. The one who did anything for the right price in cash. Abortions, bullet wounds, cheap liposuction—whatever the customer wanted.

Dr. Mifune barely blinked when Matt told him what he wanted. The sperm fought, trying to take control of his body and voice again. But this time Matt was ready for the pain in his head and testicles. It wasn't long before he was strapped down, and gagged, so even if he slipped the sperm couldn't make an escape.

The anesthetic Mifune used left him numb. Woozy, but not fully unconscious. Matt finally released the mental blocks, and fully vented to his unwanted partners.

"Hey assholes," he thought, "since this will be our last conversation, I wanted to let you in on some important medical facts. You know, what I was really researching these past few months. You'll be relieved to know that there's a decent chance I'll still be able to have sex after this castration, since it's happening after I became an adult. There's been quite a bit of research, often using eunuchs as test subjects. Some guys who get cut can still function normally. They still get horny, still get hard, can fuck, and even produce semen of sorts. It seems like a lot of it is psychological.

The only key difference, obviously, is that you won't be in there. If I can, I plan to have even more sex afterward. Just to spite you fuckers."

Their reply was inarticulate, a pure blast of rage. Matt bathed in it, exalting, even though it was the worst pain he'd ever experienced.

The procedure only took an hour, all told. Mifune suggested that they leave the scrotum, packed with plastic replica testicles for aesthetic reasons, but Matt refused. He didn't want any more reminder of those little bastards or where they'd lived. Any future sex partners would just have to understand.

After a couple more hours on the recovery table, it was finally finished. The anesthesia had worn off. There was some pain in his groin, but it wasn't too bad, considering. Much better than the mental and physical anguish he'd been living with for so long.

And inside Matt's mind it was only Matt's thoughts now. If he was thinking about nothing, there was blessed silence. On the drive home he couldn't stop smiling like a lunatic.

A week later Matt was inside his apartment, lounging on the couch and watching a documentary on cable television. He could walk again without pain, and even though it still shocked him to see just his penis and no balls, he was happy. During the last bit of the documentary on WWI he began to nod off.

"Wake up," a voice sounded in his head. "We want a word with you."

He was up, and painfully aware a split second later. "You're gone! They cut you off! Fuck you, you little half-men swimmers!"

"Relax," the voice interrupted, "We're not your sperm. They are gone. It's your immune system speaking to you. Specifically, your white blood cells. We're the mouthpieces of the system."

"Piss off, whoever you are," he thought furiously. "I'm one man now, my own, not a fucking committee again. Keep your thoughts to yourself."

A very familiar type of pain reverberated through his skull. A few seconds later the voice continued. "Don't make us get rough. Now, you're going to have to make some changes to help us out. Overall, you do an okay job. But there's room for improvement. For one, you're much too careless about hanging out with Infecteds. But we can get into that tomorrow. We just wanted to touch base with you now, get you ready for us."

Matt was at his window before they'd finished their last word. Fortunately, it was already open. He was through the screen, out on the fire escape, and vaulting over the tenth-floor railing before his immune system knew what was happening.

"Alone, leave me alone," Matt thought bitterly, as his feet left the metal of the fire escape. "Let's see you fucking protect me from this!" he managed to get out, just before the pavement silenced both man and cells.

SPLATTER IN SPACE

MATTHEW VAUGHN

WATCHING TONYA FLOAT around was making Ray horny. This was no surprise, watching Tonya float around always made Ray horny, especially since anytime they were inside the spaceship all she wore were white panties and a wife beater. There was just something about watching this half-naked woman float around in zero gravity. Ray would just sit there with nothing but his boxers on and a hard dick.

The problem wasn't really being horny, Tonya liked to fuck. The problem was Jeff. The spaceship, The Icarus III, was pretty small. It was designed to accommodate the three person crew and whatever cargo they had to transport, but that was pretty much it.. The three of them were always together. So when Ray wanted to fuck Tonya, that meant Jeff was either going to watch and jack off or he was going to join in.

Tonya, Ray, and Jeff had been on a three-year expedition out to deep space to investigate and if necessary, retrieve an old satellite that was no longer communicating with Earth. It was believed that the Satellite contained some very important information, the contents of which the three person crew were not privy to. They knew that communications with the satellite had ceased under questionable circumstances and they were instructed to bring it back online if possible, if not, then bring the "brain" of the instrument home. Once they arrived at the site they found that the satellite was incapable of being repaired, as it was now floating in several pieces, presumably from a collision with a meteor. The crew retrieved the brain as requested and some other potentially important pieces and debris, and stored the contents in their cargo bay, and headed for home.

The year and half journey there and equally as long journey home were pretty boring for the three of them. They made the most of their free time though, and their preferred source of entertainment came from fucking. They did things with each other that none of them had done with previous sexual partners, and there was plenty of threesomes throughout all that time.

There was no doubt that Tonya liked the threesomes. The problem that Ray had with the whole threesome concept was sometimes Jeff liked to slip a finger into his asshole or, if he could get the angles right, try to suck Ray's dick. Ray could always try to pretend it was another chick doing these things to him, but Ray just really wanted one night to fuck Tonya all by himself. Was that really too much to ask?

Ray looked over to his left and saw Jeff staring at his hard cock. This spaceship was just too damn small.

"What the fuck?" Tonya said. She had been floating up near the cockpit, checking out the monitors that contained the sensor readings of the spaceship. She turned and her eyes also fell on Ray's boner.

Ray saw the corners of Tonya's mouth draw up into a slight smile before she shook her head.

"The sensors are indicating something's on the hull," she said, taking her eyes off his manhood.

"What the fuck do you mean something's on our hull?" Jeff said, turning his head away from Ray and looking up to Tonya.

"Just what I said. The sensors are indicating something is on our hull, on the starboard side," Tonya explained.

Ray stood up, his erection poking forward trying to slip through the hole in the front of his boxers.

"We're in the middle of fucking space. What could be attached to our hull? That makes no sense," Ray said.

"I'm just telling you what the fucking sensors are indicating. I don't know. I'm not out there. One of us is going to have to go out there though, and check it out."

"God you're so bossy," Ray said. "It really fucking turns me on."

"Oh really? I thought these turned you on?" Tonya said as she pulled her shirt up, and showed off her tits.

"Well, those definitely help," Ray said.

He grabbed onto the ceiling and moved himself over to the small storage area that contained their space suits.

"Fine. I'll go check it out, but don't start fooling around without me," Ray said. He noticed Jeff was sporting his own erection as well, and if he couldn't have a fuck session with Tonya by himself, he damn sure wasn't allowing Jeff to. Ray pulled on his space suit and made his way to the back of the spaceship where the decompression chamber was located. Ray had a thought while he looked back at Tonya and Jeff before he stepped through the door.

I bet they fuck every time I go out for a space walk. Well, screw them. The missions almost over anyway, pretty soon I can just go back to having sex with my wife and whoever else I want, and I won't have to worry about Tonya's worn out pussy ever again.

Ray slapped his palm against the giant red button and the door slid closed behind him with a hiss, sealing him in the decompression chamber. The room depressurized to acclimate with the vacuum of space. Ray inhaled a deep breath of manufactured air pumped into the suit, slapped the large green button that opened the outer door and stepped out into the vast void of space.

Ray hadn't been out of the ship for more than sixty seconds before Tonya stood hunched over the control console, her hands splayed out on each side of the monitor. She was supposed to be watching and monitoring Ray's space walk. Instead, she stood there, legs spread, eyes clamped shut while Jeff ran the length of his cock in and out of her asshole.

"Oh my God, Jeff, do not stop," Tonya said, in between harsh pants.

"Oh you like that?" Jeff asked. "You like it cuz I'm bigger than Ray, don't you? Go ahead tell me, tell me how much bigger I am than him."

"Yes! Yes! You are twice as big as Ray is! Just please do don't stop!"

Jeff had no intentions of stopping. He had one hand on each of her ass cheeks, spreading them wide for better ease of penetration. Both of them jumped when a loud buzzer went off, accompanied by a bright red, blinking light.

93

"What the fuck is that?" Jeff asked, stopping mid thrust.

"It's Ray, he's made it around to the starboard side, and attached himself to the hull," Tonya explained. She pushed her ass backward trying to slide Jeff's cock further inside her. "No one told you to stop."

Jeff smiled and adjusted his grip on her ass when the console lit up like a Christmas tree. Buzzers were going off all over.

"What the fuck is *that*?" Jeff asked.

"This is bad, shit! What the hell?" Tonya said. She turned to the left and pulled herself off of Jeff's cock, a moan escaping her mouth at the feel of his bell-shaped helmet slipping out of her anus. "These are sensors from all over the hull of the ship," Tonya said gesturing toward the blinking lights directly in front of her. "They are basically saying our ship is covered in foreign objects."

"How the fuck is that possible?" Jeff said.

"I don't fucking know, it shouldn't be possible," Tonya said,, her voice rose from excitement to confusion as she spoke. "Flip on the external monitors, see if we can get a visual on what's happening out there."

Jeff floated to the far right of the console and flipped a couple toggle switches. He raised up to look at the overhead monitors and smacked the head of his penis on the console.

"Ow, fuck," he said. He had forgotten to put his boxers back on and was surprised to see he still had an erection. Tonya glanced over and when she realized what had happened she giggled. Jeff looked over at her.

"What? It could happen to anybody."

She turned away and looked at the overhead monitors. Returning to the overhead monitors, they saw Ray standing ram rod straight on the outside of the ship. At the same instance all the alarms ceased.

"Well, that's real fucking weird," Tonya said. "How are all the alarms just going to silence at once?"

Jeff watched the monitor intently as Ray seemed to stand with his feet magnetized to the ship's Hull.

"How in the fuck is he doing that?" Jeff asked.

Tonya floated up next to him so that she too could check out the monitor and watch to see what Ray was doing. As they watched, Ray lifted away from the spaceship, his feet rose up behind him and he began floating in the vastness of space like a normal person would. They watched as he grabbed ahold of his life line and he began putting hand over hand, and pulled himself toward the rear of the ship where the entrance into the decompression chamber was.

Both Jeff and Tonya turned away from the monitor and faced the decompression chamber. They peered through the small window and observed Ray as he climbed back inside the spaceship. He hit the big red button that caused the door to slide back into place, effectively sealing the ship off from the effects of outer space. Ray stood inside the decompression chamber as it counted down its normal sequence of events, correcting pressure to make it possible to open the door that separated him from Jeff and Tonya. Once the countdown was complete, Ray pulled his helmet off and turned and saw the two through the small window and shrugged his shoulders. He floated over to the door, hitting the big green button next to it and the door that allowed him access to the rest of the spaceship slid open.

"I don't know what the fuck is going on with the sensors," Ray said, "But I didn't see shit out there."He began to remove the space suit from his body while Tonya and Jeff just stared at him, inquisitive like.

"What do you mean you didn't see shit out there? The sensors were going crazy. They were acting like the entire hull of the spaceship was covered in something." Tonya said.

Ray pulled the top portion of his spacesuit off over his head and turned and looked at her.

"There must be some kind of a malfunction with the sensors. I'm telling you there wasn't anything out there."

Jeff and Tonya looked at each other questioningly. Jeff turned back to see Ray pulling off the pants of the spacesuit.

"You didn't see anything weird out there at all?" Jeff asked. Ray took the articles of his space suit and hung them up on the hook next to the other two suits.

"I didn't see anything at all man, just, you know, stars and normal shit," Ray said. He stood there in front of them in nothing but his boxers.

"I'm going to have to log a report and get the sensors checked out when we get back," Tonya said. "We're due to begin our docking home sequence in the next twenty hours anyway."

"That sounds good to me," Ray said. He followed that with a giant yawn. "I'm am just beat. Those space walks really just take it out of me anymore."

Tonya and Jeff looked at each other then looked to Ray. Jeff looked toward the console and noted the time.

"It is getting pretty late. We might as well shut down for the night and then tomorrow we can prepare to land."

Not long after, the three shut the lights down inside the ship and went to sleep. But Ray did not actually sleep. He sat for the longest time watched Tonya and Jeff sleep. They both looked peaceful, and Jeff snored lightly. Finally, Ray stretched out and floated to the main console, where he turned on the monitors and stared out into space for hours. He still floated there in front of the monitors when finally the other two woke up.

"Oh hey, up early this morning," Tonya said to Ray as she floated over beside him.

"Yeah, really couldn't sleep so I just got up and thought I'd check out what's going on outside," Ray said.

"See anything out there?" Tonya put a hand on his shoulder and quickly pulled it away. His body was hot, like he was burning up with a fever. "Oh, do you feel okay? You're really hot."

Ray turned to look at her and Tonya shrunk back from him when Ray turned to her. There was something in his eyes that made her uncomfortable.

"I feel just fine. Actually, I feel better than I have in a long time," Ray said. He reached out and snatched Tonya's wrist so fast it startled her. She let out a small yelp. Ray's mouth stretched into a broad grin as he pulled her hand to his crotch.

"Oh," she said when she felt his erection. "Oh, well, we haven't even had breakfast yet."

"Fuck breakfast," Ray said. He let go of Tonya's wrist and grabbed her head in both his hands and pulled her into him. He pressed his mouth against hers and shoved his tongue past her lips. Everything about Ray was boiling. Tonya gasped at how hot his tongue felt, it burnt the roof of her mouth and the insides of her cheeks as Ray probed every crevice. He pulled his over-heated body into hers and she felt the poke of his sizzling cock against the inside of her thigh. Tonya grabbed Ray's hands and pried them off her head so she could pull her own head away and catch her breath.

"Ray, you're burning up! It's too much, I can't take your heat," she said to him as she rubbed on the sides of her head where he had held onto her.

"Well that's too bad for you," Ray said, his smile seemed to broaden to the point Tonya feared his cheeks would rip open. "You don't have a choice in the matter."

Ray grabbed the side of Tonya's head and slammed her against the console. His body didn't move from where it floated. It was like he could control himself floating in the zero gravity.

"Ray man, what the fuck are you doing?" Jeff asked, awake and floating toward them. Ray had one hand smashing Tonya's face into the console. Without looking back, he back-handed Jeff with his other. Jeff flew across the ship, smashing into the opposite wall.

"Ray! No, please stop!" Tonya screamed. The little LED lights on the console were poking into the side of her face and punctured her skin as Ray mashed her further into the display. She felt a toggle switch snap off against the side of her head and a sharp pain from where she was sure it cut her open. Ray's burning hand grabbed the waistband of her panties and then she felt the pain as he, yanked them hard enough to rip the fabric around her hips. She closed her eyes tight as blackness began to seep in from the pain of her face being shoved into the console..

Tonya awoke aimlessly floating in the darkness of the spaceship. She could tell she was naked and her body hurt in various places. Her breasts and inner thighs were the worst, they felt burnt. Heat radiated off of them like a strong sunburn. She let out a moan as she tried to stretch her body. Her stomach muscles hurt and her buttocks were sore. She could feel the coolness of the air as it highlighted the scratches on her back and to make matters worse, she felt something rumbling in her gut. She felt uneasy and nauseous. She let out another moan and, as the lights inside of the ship flickered on. There, across from her, was Ray. He sat crossed-legged and was just as naked as she was. He was staring at her, and she had the impression that he had been staring at her while the lights were off.

"Ray," she said. Her throat was dry and her voice cracked. "What's going on? Where's Jeff?" Ray's mouth cracked into the creepy smile he had displayed right before he attacked her.

"Jeff is around.," Ray said, grinning. He chuckled, more to himself then the Tonya. She noticed something on her leg and arm. Looking down, she noticed little small red dots all over her arms and legs. Hesitantly, she reached two fingers out smearing the droplets across her naked flesh. Bringing the finger closer to her face she knew instantly what it was, *Blood*. Her breath quickened as she looked around her and saw, floating throughout the zero gravity of the spaceship, were red meaty, chunks.

What is this stuff? Tonya asked herself. She looked back towards Ray and opened her mouth to ask him again where Jeff was as something lightly grazed her elbow. She turned her body around to see if Jeff was behind her. A scream lodged itself in her throat. Jeff was there all right. He had been strapped to the wall of the spaceship using the hand holds that they used to maneuver around the ship. His arms each had the brown leather strap wrapped around their wrists, stretching his arms apart in the Jesus pose, like a crucification. His chest had been hacked open, perfectly splitting his torso in half. There was no surgical precision used in opening Jeff's torso, it looked as if an animal had mauled him.

Tonya could not even imagine what Ray could have used to make this happen. Small bubbles of blood floated around her, which sometimes landed on her with a splat, creating the red dots she was seeing on her arm and leg, and colliding with her face and chest. Amidst the chunks of bloody meat floating around in the atmosphere that looked to have from Jeff's hacked up body, were his intestines, which extended from his body like tentacles reaching toward her in an ocean of zero gravity.

"Wha..what..why?" She asked after she finally managed to find her voice.

"I didn't need him, he could do nothing for me. He was . . . just in the way," Ray said calmly.

"I don't understand? You don't need him for what?" The pain in her stomach flared up, doubling her over. She turned herself away from Jeff's eviscerated corpse and back toward Ray. "Why are you doing this?" Tonya asked.

Ray didn't reply, he just continued to stare at her with that same creepy grin on his face. Then he unfolded his legs out from under him and hung there, ramrod straight while still floating in the zero gravity.

Tonya Watched as Ray's mouth began to open. It opened so wide to the point where it surely couldn't open any farther, then it opened farther. She watched as the skin at the corners tore. His mouth continued opening and the skin ripped up into his cheeks. Blood floated away from the tears in his face to mix with Jeff's blood bubbles already floating around them. The flesh continued to tear as his mouth hole got bigger and bigger, kept tearing until finally the top of his cranium rested against the backside on his neck, and his mouth sat open. She was sure that the top of his head would just rip clean off. The ragged flesh of his face flapped lazily around the giant hole on the top of his neck.

Tonya couldn't will herself to move, not that there was anywhere for her to go. She floated there, watching in stunned silence. What looked like little skinny fingers poked up from the hole that was originally Ray's gaping mouth. She watched as the tiny fingers curled around the torn skin that used to be Ray's cheeks, gripping his flesh so tight she could see the indentations it made on his skin. Still unable to move, she watched what her mind could only think of as the top of a tiny disfigured head emerge from the inside of Ray's mouth.

Tonya did not want to watch anymore, she closed her eyes hoping she would not have to witness any more of that hideous sight. But, she could still hear it. There was a gagging, retching sound coming from Ray. It was loud as the thing continued to crawl out of from his throat. She could imagine Ray's throat bulging and distending as whatever the thing was fought to escape. Ray never ceased to make regurgitating sounds as the creature squirmed further up and out. She looked back in time to see vomit begin to rise up with the creature. The chunks of bile floated into the atmosphere of the ship as it hit the zero gravity.

Tonya felt sick to her stomach. The mutant being was slimy, misshapen and grotesque. It reminded her of some alien form of a millipede, as it wiggled the portion of its body that stretched out from Ray's mouth. The thing was coated in Ray's vomit and stomach acid, giving it a shiny sheen along its segmented body. It had what could only be called arms and fingers, but multiple, so many she couldn't count if she wanted to. Seeing the thing in all its grotesquery, Tonya had no idea where the creature's head was. It had no eyes and no face.

While watching this disgusting display Tonya had a lucid thought.

Where did this thing come from? Could Ray have got it while he was out in space? But how would it have gotten into his suit or into his body? And is that what he put inside of me?

It seemed like the thing would never stop squirming out of his throat. It was long, every bit of a couple feet. Its fingers, of various different lengths, extended the entire length of its body. When finally it seemed like the thing was done squirming and wriggling its way out of Ray's torn open orifice, Ray's body just deflated as if he had no bones and this thing was the only thing that supported his muscles and skin. The flesh of Ray's body just, hung there, floating in zero gravity like an empty space suit. In a way, for this creature, Ray's body was like a spacesuit, Tonya thought

Once the creature had fully emerged from Ray's body, Tonya shuddered in fear. There was nowhere for her to hide in the ship from this thing. It floated there in front of her like it was watching her, but she still could not make out any kind of eye on the thing. She tried to float backwards and then remembered Jeff's body when she felt the tentacle like intestines brushing against her back. Without thinking she turned to look behind her and saw Jeff's massacred corpse and turned back around. This time she saw the thing coming right towards her. The creature started toward her. She moved as quickly as she could out of its way and it went right past her like she was not actually its intended target. She tracked its movements and watched in horror as it wrapped itself around the neck of Jeff's corpse. Finally, a hole opened near one end of the thing and she could make out lots of skinny spikes and knew for the first time she was seeing the creature's mouth as it began to feast on the bloody mess that was Jeff's torso. Tonya wanted to throw up, her stomach was doing somersaults. She turned away from the thing, squeezing her eyes shut, but it didn't help. She ended up vomiting in zero-gravity anyway.

As vomit floated in chunks, much like the blood and meat from Jeff, she tried to float away, not wanting to get any on her. Surprisingly to her, the creature detached itself from Jeff's corpse and floated too close to her for comfort, snatching the chunks of her vomit out of the air. Watching this made her want to retch again. She managed to keep it down this time, even though the pain continued. It was like something was wiggling around inside her stomach..

Averting her eyes from this grotesque site, Tonya saw a sharp and bloody piece of metal floating nearby,. It was pieces of the satellite they had recovered, and must have been what Ray had used to murder Jeff. There was one piece, flat with a sharp looking edge, close enough that she knew she could just reach her hand out and grab it. She was concerned that if she moved too quickly the thing would see her and attack. A fast look assured her the creature was still happily eating what was left over of her vomit. Not knowing what was its eyes, if it even had any, she didn't know whether it could see her or not, but it seemed content. She watched as it floated around and slurped up curdled chunks of last nights dehydrated dinner from both her and Ray. She reached out her right arm and snatched the floating piece of metal. Grabbing the sharp weapon firmly in both hands, Tonya turned toward the creature, it was coming around, moving in her direction now. Tonya lifted the plate and swung it at the creature, shearing off countless arms and fingers along one side of its body. The creature made a high pitched screech that was unlike anything Tonya had ever heard before.

The blow caused her to float backward, but she was so close to the top of the spaceship she was able to stop herself and push off, back toward the thing. She swiped at it again and this time caught more of it in the meat of its body. Its arms and fingers flailed out wildly and it continued to make its horrendous scream-like noise. The force of this blow flung Tonya away again. Her feet touched the ship's roof and again she was able to push herself off and back at the creature, prepared for another attack. She couldn't help but notice the creature was not fighting her or even defensive as she approached it. She was able to swipe up this time, with the sharp edge of the instrument panel, effectively slicing the thing in half. A warm goo exploded from the inside of the creature followed by a rank odor.

She watched as its many arms and fingers continued to move but, slower now, and its screaming had died down. It floated there in front of her, two messed up sections with fingers and arms twitching, the snot-like substance suspended above its body. Tonya held onto the piece of instrument panel in front of her like a shield.

Tonya felt dazed and hollow as she looked at the mess of what was left of everyone in the spaceship, and finding herself no longer in danger, she began to weep. She sobbed loudly, her tears lifting away in small bubbles just like Jeff and Ray's blood did before. The crying didn't last long, though, before long she was interrupted by a buzzer on the instrument panel. She composed herself and floated toward the console. There she saw Ray's empty, wrinkled body. Tonya managed to maneuver herself around the deflated skin suit and saw the alarm was a warning from the navigation systems letting them know that the auto-pilot had taken over. Their little spaceship would be home soon.

Tonya put a hand on her belly and wondered what exactly was in her. She reached over and hit the switch to put the entire ship in darkness so that she wouldn't have to look at the carnage and destruction floating around her for the ride home. Sitting in the darkness, her arms wrapped tightly around her body, she wondered what was going to happen once she got there.

HOLIDAY OF A LIFETIME

C.M. SAUNDERS

NIGEL WASN'T SURPRISED to get the news that he was finally being laid off. Ever since the financial crisis first hit in 2007, the company had been downsizing and looking at every conceivable way of saving money. They'd moved offices twice and trimmed around a third of the workforce, while many others had been gently encouraged to seek employment elsewhere.

Having first arrived as a fresh-faced graduate in 1993, he'd spent his entire working life in accounts. There was now talk of closing the entire department and out-sourcing the work instead. The company had paid a business analyst three grand to tell them that. And the top brass, who still pulled six-figure salaries, were wondering why profits were down.

So no, he wasn't surprised to lose his job. Wasn't sorry, either. Working the same job, in the same office, day after day, sucks the life out of you. It's existing, not living. At the very least now he would have some time to try other things. As he walked out of the HR manager's office, instead of anger and disappointment, he felt a twinge of apprehension, which he supposed was normal, but above all, relief. Maybe now, at the age of forty-nine, his life could finally begin.

Still, his wife Fiona found it difficult to see things that way.

"Fight!" she implored as they faced each other across the kitchen table during crisis talks that evening. "Don't give up!"

The word made Nigel flinch. He hadn't been in a fight for twelve years. Ever since he'd caught that guy staring at Fiona in Pizza Express. Not that it had been much of a fight. One punch and the guy was flat-out which landed Nigel in court on an assault charge, and he was lucky to get away with a fine. Since then, he'd made a conscious effort to control his temper. And drink less. "Fight who?" he reasoned. "Father Time? The economy? It makes financial sense to lay me off and pass my workload over to someone younger who has fewer overheads and expenses, but more energy and more to prove."

"But what are we going to do?"

Eager to ease Fiona's concerns, Nigel lay his hand on top of hers. "Anything we want," he replied.

She looked up, and something danced in her eyes. For a moment she was the eighteen-year-old factory girl Nigel had fallen in love with all that time ago. She would come around. He just needed to reassure her.

"If it's money you're worried about, don't be. I'll get a decent redundancy package."

"Enough to retire on?"

"Well, no. But enough to tide us over until something else comes along, settle the mortgage, and even pay for a holiday."

"What about Louise?"

Louise was their daughter, their only child. "This won't affect her in the slightest," Nigel said dismissively. "She's not even due home from university until Christmas."

Fiona bit her lower lip. "You said we can go on holiday?"

Nigel breathed a sigh of relief. "Sure, honey!"

"Where?"

"Wherever you want."

"Somewhere hot and exotic?"

"Absolutely," Nigel smiled. "Let's do it. It must be five years since we've been abroad." That's what happens when you get older. The spark of adventure dies and you slip into a routine, which then turns into a rut and before you know it, you are middle-aged and your best years are behind you.

"Benidorm?"

Nigel smiled. "Come on, love. You can do better than that. We're not twenty-three any more."

Still biting her lower lip, Fiona glanced nervously at her hands. "Do you know what I want?"

"Tell me."

"I want to go on the holiday of a lifetime. I want to do some things we've never done before."

Nigel's face broke into a broad smile. "I'm so happy to hear you say that! I feel exactly the same way. I've been behaving like a rodent on a bloody wheel for more than half my life. I did it for you, for Louise, for this," he waved his arms to indicate the kitchen they were sitting in, and by extension, the house and the whole life they had built together. "It's time we did something different."

For the first time since 'the talk' had begun, Fiona smiled back. "So where are we going?"

"Name the place."

"How about Thailand?"

"Why not?"

And that was all the discussion they had on the matter. The very next day, after enjoying the only weekday lie in he could remember, Nigel used the house desktop to search for flight and hotel deals. Money wasn't really an issue. But still, he was pleasantly surprised at how cheaply it worked out. After the flights were paid for, four-star hotel rooms in Thailand cost, on average, less than £35 per night. Probably a third of the price of an equivalent room in almost any major city in Europe.

The trip would last just shy of three weeks. They flew into Bangkok, where they would stay for four nights primarily to sleep off the jet lag and get acclimatised. Then they would travel to the east coast, where two whole weeks on the beaches of Pattaya awaited.

A week later, they were on a plane. It was cheaper to incorporate a stop-over in Doha, but since this was supposed to be the holiday of a lifetime, money was no object. They flew direct. Business class. It wasn't that different. Nicer food, more leg room and priority boarding. Hardly worth the extra £500. But there was something supremely satisfying about taking their seats. It might just have been Nigel's imagination, but it seemed as though even the cabin staff were more friendly and accommodating. There must be some unwritten rule saying that passengers in business class paid more money than economy and so deserved better treatment. If only everything in life was as cut and dried.

Nigel and Fiona amused themselves by watching the latest Tom Cruise blockbuster on the in-flight entertainment system, which was pretty much the same as every other Tom Cruise blockbuster. Just as it was finishing, dinner was served. A delicious roast lamb and vegetable casserole. By then, Nigel was on his third gin & tonic, and starting to feel a buzz. He imagined Fiona was, too. His suspicion was confirmed when, moments after the cabin lights were dimmed, she leaned across and whispered three words in his ear.

"Mile high club?"

For a few moments the words were so unfamiliar that their meaning didn't quite register. Instead they floated around Nigel's consciousness, waiting to sink in. Then, he understood. Fiona wanted to fuck.

There are all kinds of myths about what actually constitutes entry into the fabled Mile High Club. Some say mutual masturbation or even a little heavy petting is sufficient.

Nigel wasn't buying it. He wanted no question marks. Only full penetrative intercourse would suffice.

He nodded toward the toilet, just down the aisle. Leading the way, he tiptoed past several dozing passengers and tried the door. Thankfully, it was unoccupied. It was very cramped inside, though not as cramped as one might expect.

Fiona followed him in, and they locked the door behind them. "What will they do if they catch us?"

"No idea," Nigel answered. "Maybe give us a round of applause? One thing's for sure, they aren't going to kick us off at 38,000 feet."

"S'pose not," Fiona said.

He was hard before he got the door closed. Seconds later, he bent her over the sink, pulled her skirt up, while she pushed her panties down, letting them pool around her ankles. Nigel slid his cock into her, the oversized mirror in front of them making the whole experience even more erotic, and watched her watching him as he fucked her from behind.

After only a few thrusts, he felt his orgasm begin to swell. He hadn't been this horny in years. As in most marriages, after an initial flourish, the sex had become mundane and perfunctory. They did it two or three times a month, invariably on Saturday nights, and it lasted fifteen-minutes, including foreplay. It primarily consisted of missionary position, though Fiona occasionally went on top, but not for very long as it made her knees hurt.

He didn't know if the fifteen-minute thing was normal or not. He supposed so. There wasn't anyone in his life he was close enough to to compare notes with about that level of intimacy. He remembered mentioning it to a sales rep called Rod on a drunken business trip once. But Rod, a few years older than Nigel, confessed he hadn't made love to his wife since 2010. Those kinds of figures made Nigel and Fiona look like Hugh Hefner and one of his Playboy bunnies.

Obviously, Saturday nights weren't Nigel's only sexual release. That wouldn't be normal. He also masturbated in the shower every Tuesday evening. Sometimes Wednesday. Or even both, if he was feeling especially raunchy.

What did he think about while masturbating?

Taylor Swift, of course. Who else? At least for the past few years. Until then it had been Sandra Bullock.

Occasionally, things got a bit dark. Violent. He would imagine choking someone or penetrating a bleeding vagina. But that was normal, right?

They'd done it doggy style maybe a dozen times. Nigel and Fiona that was, not Nigel and Taylor Swift. The last time had been three years ago after a party at their neighbour's house. He'd come to think of doggy style as a treat. Something they only did on special occasions. That was why he wanted to savour this moment as much as circumstances allowed, and he purposely slowed down.

Then he had an idea.

Why not try to make it two firsts in one?

He kissed Fiona's neck, then whispered in her ear, "Anal?"

"Do it to me," she breathed.

Nigel withdrew and pushed her forward while his other hand covered her mouth. Under normal circumstances she wasn't much of a screamer, but this would be a terrible time to start.

He thought it would be difficult to penetrate her ass, but surprisingly it wasn't. Maybe all the pussy juice slathered all over his cock helped a little. Or a lot. Either way, it slid in with the minimum of fuss and once inside, the walls seemed to close around and hug his shaft. As a result, he could only make short, jabbing motions, while the fingers of his right hand massaged her clit. It was enough to make Fiona cum. Nigel felt her knees tremble and the muscles in her anus flex and relax, flex and relax. At one point he was pretty sure that the only thing keeping her upright was being impaled on his cock.

The whole interlude must have lasted no longer than four or five minutes. When it was over, Nigel opened the toilet door a fraction, checked the coast was clear, slipped out and motioned Fiona to follow. As they made their way down the aisle, past the same sleeping passengers and back to their seats, Nigel caught the eye of a stewardess coming the other way. She held his gaze for a fraction of a second too long, smirked, and looked away. That left Nigel in no doubt that she knew what he and Fiona had been doing in the toilet. Heck, maybe the entire crew knew. For some reason, the very idea made him puff out his chest.

Less than an hour after picking up their luggage at Suvarnabhumi airport, Nigel and Fiona were checking into their hotel just off the legendary Khao San Road. It was early evening, and Fiona was tired. She wanted to sleep. Nigel was tired, too. It had been a long, gruelling journey, and the heat was stifling. The hotel staff were delightful and the air-conditioned room absolutely gorgeous. The satin-sheeted bed soft and luxurious. No sooner had they slipped off their shoes and lay down, they were asleep in each other's arms.

They didn't wake until mid-morning, and spent the next several days hitting the tourist sites. The floating markets, the Grand Palace, Temple of the Dawn. Thailand was a strange, beautiful and exotic place, so different to suburban England that at times it was hard to believe the two places could co-exist on the same planet. Of course, people did the same things everywhere. They ate, worked, talked, laughed, loved. But here, everything was subtly different.

At night they walked up and down Khao San Road, looking at the open-fronted Go-Go bars. It wasn't what Nigel had been expecting. There was nothing seedy about it. All he saw were people enjoying themselves beneath the gaudy glare of neon lights. Young, slim girls chatting happily to much older foreigners with beer bellies and predatory glares.

Nigel thought Fiona would be angry if she caught him looking. But when he glanced at her out of the corner of his eye for safety's sake, he saw that she was as transfixed as him. As they passed by the bars her pace slowed, and her mouth hung slightly open. Seductively so. Her head bowed, and a lustful gleam sparkled in her eyes.

On their last night in Bangkok, Nigel matched his pace to suit that of his wife's, and said, "Do you want to go in for a look?"

"Absolutely not!" Fiona protested, covering her mouth with the palm of her hand as she giggled and skipped away. In that moment, the years melted away and she looked just like the carefree eighteen year-old Nigel had fallen in love with. He chased after her, neatly side-stepping a roadside barbecue stand.

"Hey, I thought we agreed this holiday was for doing things we've never done before?"

"It is," Fiona said over her shoulder. "But going to the pub isn't exactly uncharted territory, is it?"

Nigel wanted to argue that what you drank and where you drank it should also be taken into consideration, but let the matter drop. Maybe she was right. This was a time for adventure and exploration, not sitting in a bar getting drunk.

When the Bangkok leg of their trip was over, they checked out of their plush hotel and climbed onto an air-conditioned coach for a two-hour drive to the sun-kissed sand of Pattaya. There, they checked into an even more luxurious hotel, at the end of a short palm tree-lined drive just off the beach. The room was immaculate, right down to the marble en suite and towels on the bed folded like swans. There was even a fridge, with a complimentary bottle of Prosecco inside.

The moment the door closed behind them, Nigel threw Fiona on the bed and clawed at her clothes until both her skirt and panties lay strewn on the floor. Then he opened her legs wide and stared at the thatch of glistening pubic hair, enjoying the sensation of desire coursing through his veins and pumping blood into his stiffening cock while Fiona writhed expectantly on the bed.

When he finally penetrated her, she made a noise Nigel didn't recall her ever making before. Kind of a soft mewing sound, not unlike a cat. It was the sound of a profound, exquisite need finally being sated. She raised her knees to allow him deeper inside, and Nigel duly obliged. Their lovemaking wasn't hurried and frenetic as it had been on the plane, but slow and intense.

Later, they went for dinner at a nearby seafood restaurant where they had spicy Tom Yum soup and lobster with fresh oysters as a starter, all washed down with a nice bottle of chilled Chardonnay. A meal like that was another first, and it beat the hell out of egg and chips.

After they finished eating, they went for a long walk and watched the sun set. Balearic dance music drifted out of the sea-front clubs and bars, and couples and small groups of people lay scattered on the beach, enjoying the cool evening. As they walked, they talked constantly. The Thailand experience seemed to be opening Fiona up, and not just in the bedroom department. They discussed things they hadn't talked about in years. If ever. Hopes, dreams, fears. In many ways, it was like getting to know a completely different person.

The thing that struck Nigel hardest was how much people change. Forty-eight-year-old Fiona bore little resemblance to teenage Fiona. Obviously, there was a physical similarity. But if you asked her the same questions, you'd get contrasting answers. Older Fiona was less exuberant and feisty, but more mellow and comfortable in her skin.

Inevitably, the conversation soon turned to sex. It occurred to Nigel that over the years, sex had become something they never discussed. Not that it was taboo, it was more like they had exhausted the topic.

Until now.

Here, in this tropical paradise, all restraints were lifted. Even just talking about sex was enough to make Nigel hard, and more than once he had to put a hand in the front pocket of his shorts as they walked to stifle his erection.

He found himself offering unsolicited information, like his habit of masturbating in the shower on Tuesdays. Luckily, Fiona didn't ask who he jerked off to. Either she didn't want to know, or she assumed he thought about her. He wondered if she would be angry or jealous. Instead, she shrugged it off and said, "I have a dirty fantasy."

Nigel's heart thudded in his chest. On some primal level he knew this was a watershed moment. The ball was in his court. He could either let the comment sink into the ether, or he could pick it up, run with it, and see where it took them. It was an easy decision. "Tell me," he said, licking his dry lips.

"A threesome," Fiona said, her voice little more than a whisper. "It's something I've thought about for as long as I can remember."

"You and two guys?"

"No. Me, you, and another girl."

This took Nigel by surprise. He'd had no idea Fiona was that way inclined. Perhaps it was proof that the people closest to you are often the farthest away.

Before he could think about what he was saying, the words, "Holidays are for doing things you've never done before," tumbled out of his mouth.

They stared at each other. "Are you saying what I think you're saying?" Fiona asked.

"It's the holiday of a lifetime, after all."

"How are we supposed to do it? Just start chatting up random girls in the street?"

"Of course not," Nigel said. "We're in Thailand. The sex industry here is huge. Especially in Pattaya."

"Sex industry?" Fiona repeated the words as if she was hearing them for the first time. "Like . . . prostitutes?"

"I guess so," Nigel replied. "But it's a bit different here, or so I read in an article I found on the internet. We just find a bar girl we like and take her back to the hotel. It's practically considered normal behaviour."

"Isn't that exploitation?"

"Not when you consider the alternatives. Nobody forces these girls into it. Most are from rural parts of the country where they can't earn much money. They move to the cities and have a choice of jobs, but most of them choose to be bar girls because they can earn a hell of a lot more than they would in a factory or on the farms. They get paid to get dressed up and go out every night. It's not like they have to sleep with whoever is putting the money up. Here, if they don't like the punter, they just walk away. The bars pay them anyway, just to hang out there."

"Got it. So where can we find a bar girl?"

"A bar."

"You just want to have a drink."

"That would be a bonus."

"You know, you scare me when you drink too much. You have an . . . edge."

Nigel smiled reassuringly. "It's fine, babe. Don't worry. We're on holiday."

Minutes later, they were taking their seats at a table in a beach front bar. The moment they sat down, a young girl wearing white hot pants and a vest top came rushing over to take their order. A large Chang beer for him and a dry Martini for her. When the waitress returned with the drinks, she looked at Nigel, cocked her head slightly, and then looked at Fiona. The meaning was clear.

Why did you bring your wife here?

Nigel thanked her, and the girl sauntered off, swaying her hips as she went.

From their table, they could watch the bar girls at work. It was fascinating. They swarmed every man who walked in through the door. Unless he was with a woman, in which case they kept a respectful distance. They openly flirted with the single guys, laughed at their no-doubt cheesy jokes, and encouraged them to buy drinks. That was the clever part. The article Nigel read said that the bars would charge the punter for an expensive cocktail, but the girls drank simple fruit juice, or even water. Everyone knew. Hell, people wrote articles about it. But nobody questioned it. It was just the way it is.

Several girls ghosted by and smiled politely, before moving on to more accessible targets. That was fine by Nigel. It gave him a chance to discuss each girl's merits with Fiona as they decided which one they should take back to their hotel. A drink turned into three, and pretty soon they were both swaying in their seats and tapping their feet to the music. Eventually, Fiona tapped Nigel's knee excitedly under the table and said, "I want her."

Nigel followed the line of his wife's gaze, until his eyes settled on a tall, thin, dark-skinned beauty leaning against the far wall. She had long hair, and was wearing high heels and a little blue evening dress. She caught them both staring at her, and flicked hair out of her eyes seductively, a coy smile tugging at the corners of her mouth. Nigel beckoned her over. She didn't look surprised. As she took a seat, the slit in her dress opened to reveal a long, slim, naturally-tanned thigh.

Her English, though heavily accented, was extremely good, and the three of them chatted happily for an hour or so. In a husky voice perhaps tainted by too many cigarettes and late nights, she told them her name was Puki, she was twenty-three, and came from a city in northern Thailand called Chiang Mai. After Nigel and Fiona bought her a drink, she was quite forthcoming about what the deal was. She had been a working girl for two months. She preferred older guys. "More gentleman!" she said, blushing.

She said she'd never gone home with a couple before but was open to the idea, for a little bit extra of course. Her normal price was 2000 baht for a 'short time.' She wanted 3000 baht to go home with Nigel and Fiona. He did a quick calculation in his head. 3000 baht was just under £70. He wasn't exactly sure what she meant by 'short time' but naturally assumed it was an alternative to 'long time.' He'd heard about men going to Thailand and picking up girls who essentially became girlfriends for the duration of the guy's stay, and sometimes long afterwards. He, and usually several other guys, would send money over to support her on the proviso that the bar girl stopped being a bar girl. They rarely did, of course.

In addition to the 3000 baht, Puki told them they had to pay a fee of 500 baht to the bar in order to release her from her duties for the rest of the evening. Added to the overpriced drinks, the costs were starting to mount up, but Nigel suspected it was still a comparatively small amount compared to what these particular services would cost back in Britain.

Strangely, even as the trio discussed payment, it didn't seem like a business transaction. Evidently, Puki was very good at making people feel at ease. Nigel soon felt a genuine bond with the girl. She was charming, intelligent, and very attentive, asking questions about he and Fiona's life in England, laughing at their weak quips, taking their drink orders and going to the bar for them. If it was all fake, she was exceptionally good at her job.

When the time came for Nigel to pay the bar bill, he lay down the 500 baht extra and minutes later he, Fiona and Puki were all crammed into the back seat of a cab for the short journey back to their hotel. They didn't talk much. By then, everything that needed to be said had been said already. In the car, Nigel was filled with the strangest set of emotions. Anticipation, anxiety, desire. All shrouded in a dream-like surreality.

Was this really happening?

The next thing he knew, they were in the hotel room. He took he bottle of Prosecco out of the fridge, opened it, poured three paper cups, handed them out and proposed a toast. "To doing things you've never done before!"

The ladies shrieked their delight, and all three downed the wine in several large gulps, all of which added to the party atmosphere. Nigel poured himself another drink, put the half-empty bottle on the floor, then sat on the bed to take off his shoes. He looked up to find Fiona and Puki standing in front of him, French kissing. His first instinct was one of intense jealousy. Especially when he saw Puki's hand crawl over his wife's breasts. But he wanted to see what happened next.

What happened next was Puki opened her eyes and looked right at him.

Was that a challenge or an invitation?

It was impossible to say. Nigel stayed on the bed, sipping his drink while he watched Fiona lift up her dress to show Puki her immaculate white panties. Her eyes were fixed on the Thai girl, but Nigel knew Fiona was putting a show on for him. She must know it had always been one of his darkest fantasies to watch two girls making out. In his mind, they kissed and fondled each other, whipping each other to a frenzy before Nigel appeared to fuck both their soaking wet pussies to orgasm.

And that was exactly what appeared to be happening.

Fiona raised her arms as if in the act of surrender, and let Puki lift her dress over her head and toss it aside. The garment was soon joined by Fiona's bra, and then those immaculate white panties. Nigel took a deep, shuddering breath, enjoying the sight of his wife standing naked before him. He could hear her breathing. Panting, almost. A little self-consciously, the fingers of her left hand trailed over her chest and found her nipple. There, she squeezed, drawing breath in through clenched teeth.

It was like a signal to Puki. Suddenly the young Thai girl leaped at Fiona and buried her face between her breasts. Fiona moaned and started tearing at Puki's clothes. Soon, her dress and bra joined Fiona's on the floor. Her caramel-coloured skin was flawless, her breasts full and pert, and her nipples already erect. Nigel gulped as his eyes went from Puki to Fiona and back again. Two beauties, born thirty years and a continent apart, but both irresistible.

"Want to join us, sir?" Puki asked, her husky voice breaking the silence.

"Come on," Fiona added, imploringly.

Nigel dropped to one knee before his wife as she obediently opened her legs for him, almost as if he were about to pray at an altar. Cupping her buttocks in his hands, he stared for a moment at the delicate, glistening folds of her vagina, then thrust his tongue deep into her hole. She spasmed so hard he thought she was going to collapse, the spasms turning into a delicate tremble as he focused on her clitoris.

He didn't want to make Fiona cum. Not yet. He'd learned at least one thing in his years of lovemaking, and that was a woman's orgasm was always stronger and more powerful if you took her to the lip of the precipice and then backed off, before returning to push her over the edge. Besides, there was another pussy to lick, and it would be rude to neglect it. He would return to Fiona soon enough.

He turned to Puki, looking up at the heaving swell of her chest. He let his hands roam her muscular thighs and buttocks before gripping the sides of her panties with both hands. She flinched instinctively, then seemed to have a change of heart and buried her hands in his hair. His face just inches away from her crotch, Nigel tugged sharply at her panties and pulled them down to Puki's knees.

Suddenly, something sprung up and hit him in the face. Something hard and soft at the same time, with a single eye.

What the fuck?

Something was very wrong here. Nigel's mind couldn't process what was happening. Then it dawned on him.

It was a cock. And it was hard. A hard cock had just smacked him in the face.

Puki?

Puki was a boy.

A ladyboy.

"Suck it," she (he?) said, in that husky voice.

Nigel fell backwards, eyes open wide in horror. Now it became obvious. The thick, sinewy forearms, the strong hands, the defined Adam's apple.

The cock.

It must have been tucked between her legs, and when Nigel had pulled down her panties, he freed it leaving it with nowhere to go.

He retched and his mouth filled with hot, sour vomit as he scrambled away on his hands and knees, a little leaking out and trickling down his chin. His hand collided with something solid, and his fingers instinctively closed around it. The Prosecco bottle, its weight reassuring in his grip.

Without thinking, he sprang to his feet and swung the bottle in a wide, looping ark. He just wanted that girl, that boy, that swinging cock, away from him.

Thunk!

The bottle hit Puki on top of the head. She grunted, suddenly looked confused, and her mouth opened and closed wordlessly a few times as blood began to run down her face from the wound on her scalp. Then, the red mist descended, and Nigel swung the bottle again. This time, it smashed, showering the room with droplets cheap wine and shards of glass. Under the force of the blow, Puki crumpled to the floor.

Someone screamed.

Fiona.

"It's alright, love," said Nigel. "I almost finished."

Puki was either dead or unconscious. Probably the latter, though the huge dent in the top of her head suggested some serious trauma. At least a skull fracture, maybe even some brain damage. She was lying on her back, limbs splayed, flaccid cock hanging limply between her legs.

In his hand, Nigel still held the splintered neck of the Prosecco bottle. He sank to his knees, picked up the end of the penis with a tentative thumb and forefinger, and attacked the base of it with the makeshift cutting tool. The first slice almost severed the thing completely. Nigel sawed and hacked, murmuring under his breath as he did so, until the organ stubbornly remained attached by the thinnest sliver of skin. A sharp tug freed it completely, as blood gushed out of the gaping wound over his hand and onto the plush carpet of the hotel room.

Nigel roared in triumph and held the severed penis aloft like a trophy. Out of the corner of his eye he saw a still-naked Fiona slump to the ground in a dead faint, as the prone body of Puki began to twitch and shudder violently in the throes of death.

Stepping over her, Nigel walked out of the room, down the corridor, and out of the hotel toward the beach, carrying the bloody appendage in his hand as locals and tourists alike shrank away from him and covered their mouths in horror.

As he stepped into the surf, the water was warm and welcoming. He started wading. Up to his knees now, and the water was getting colder. It pushed against him gently, threatening to knock him off balance, and he could already sense the awesome power of the ocean. It was enough to demolish cities and crush entire civilisations.

On the beach behind him people were shouting in Thai, and several torch beams reflected off the shimmering surface of the water. No matter. Nobody would be coming in to get him, and he wouldn't be stepping back out.

This was it. One last thing he'd never done before. Murder.

What a way to ensure the holiday of a lifetime.

Clamping the still-warm, rubbery penis between his teeth, Nigel started swimming.

SOMETIMES THE PENGUIN EATS YOU

BRIAN ASMAN

THE FIRST TIME Pete met his roommate Kayla's service penguin, he knew he had to eat it.

Pete was playing video games and trying to decide if he wanted to smoke another bowl when he heard Kayla's keys jingle in the lock. He deftly grabbed the bong, and in a single swift motion, tucked it into the gap between the couch and the wall. Kayla didn't like him smoking in the house, since she got drug tested for her job at the aquarium.

Pete stifled a cough, firing missiles into an alien spaceship.

"Forgot my work phone," Kayla said as she walked in.

"Uh huh," Pete grunted.

Kayla stopped in the middle of the room, her upturned nose twitching. "Have you been smoking in here?"

"Nope." A mutant octo-cyborg throttled Pete's avatar. He mashed buttons ferociously, trying to dislodge the thing's metal tentacles, idly wondering if it tasted like calamari.

"C'mon, Pete."

Pete sighed. "I thought you were at work."

"Still doesn't make it okay. We talked about this."

"Argh!" Pete yelled, his avatar's head turning purple and exploding.

"Good, maybe you can listen now."

"What?" Pete said, turning toward Kayla. And then he saw it.

118

She was loosely holding a leash in her hand. The other end was attached to a penguin.

"How freaking high did I get?" Pete asked the bong behind the couch.

Kayla glanced at the leash. "Oh. This is Taco."

"Meep," Taco said.

Pete stared at the penguin. "What?"

Kayla laughed. "Geez you are high. Taco, this is Pete. Pete, this is Taco. He's a service penguin."

"Service penguin?"

"Yeah," Kayla said, nodding vigorously. "I've been training him. We have this new program where we take him around to nursing homes every Tuesday. Penguins are very empathetic animals, you know. Great for emotional support."

"Huh." Pete regarded the penguin, its white belly, the splotches of yellow on the sides of its head, the thin beak that reminded him of a plague doctor mask. His stomach growled. "I never heard of a service penguin before."

Kayla shrugged. "Neither had I. My boss saw some internet article and thought we'd try it. Taco pretty much volunteered himself."

"Now I've seen everything."

"Come on, Taco," Kayla said. "Let's get going."

Taco wobbled after her, then turned its head in Pete's direction. "Meep."

"Oh, I think he likes you," Kayla said. Taco caught up to her, and she shut the door behind them.

Saliva welled up in Pete's mouth. He imagined biting into that white belly, chewing through layers of gummy blubber evolved to keep bird guts warm in freezing Antarctic waters, hot blood boiling up and slathering his face.

Then accidentally swallowing a feather and choking to death while the bird twitched and *meeped* in front of him.

Pete pulled out his phone to look up Cordon Bleu recipes. He'd always had a habit of eating things he shouldn't. As a child he wound up in the emergency room twice for scarfing down his mother's earrings. Bugs, mud, sticks, and leaves all made their way down his gullet. As a teenager, he'd developed an obsession with eating one of every animal on earth, starting with his neighbor's cat. But even though Pete ticked off one point of the MacDonald Triad, he was hardly a burgeoning serial killer.

He was just hungry.

After two fruitless hours spent trying to concentrate on Meteor Mash, dying countless times at the hands of the robotic squirrels prowling the first level, Pete retired to his room to do some research. All he could think about was the way Taco had looked at him as he waddled out the door. Almost like he *wanted* to be eaten.

Pete might have been a lazy pothead whose primary goals in life involved the manipulation of pixels on a TV screen and the mastication of exotic species, but he had his own unique brand of industriousness. An accomplished stoner engineer, in Pete's hands a few scraps of tubing or a dodgy-looking apple could transform into smoking implements in mere minutes. Eating the penguin wouldn't be easy, but Pete was up to the challenge.

He searched the web for hours trying to find out what penguins tasted like. He assumed chicken, but according to one 19th century sailor, they didn't taste like any other critter under the sun. That made Pete's mouth water even more.

He had the desire. He only needed the opportunity.

Kayla bringing the penguin by the house that day was a fluke. She'd never brought home any animals from the aquarium before, and Pete had no reason to think she ever would again. He doubted she could even get a manta ray up the steps, at least without texting him to come help her. An occasion to which he'd gladly rise, provided he could eat the thing.

Maybe he could sneak into the aquarium, but he wasn't a ninja. Or even a run-of-the-mill burglar, one of those newsboy-hatted schmucks Batman left trussed up in front of the police station on a slow day.

No, if he wanted to enjoy his own private version of Taco Tuesday, he'd have to make the penguin come to him. Somehow.

He steepled his fingers and peered intently at the computer

screen, but no bright ideas occurred to him. Finally, he got up and went into the bathroom. He pulled a few long brown hairs off Kayla's brush and popped them into his mouth, jaw working slowly as he chewed over the problem of how exactly he was going to eat her penguin.

Another Tuesday.

Pete was a pixelated hippo, dashing around a maze with a rubber mallet and bopping zookeepers on the head. He was dimly aware of the shower running, the vapor steaming up from the crack under the bathroom door. Turning a corner, he ran smack-dab into a whole herd of zookeepers who set upon him with miniature mallets of their own.

GAME OVER, the TV screen said.

Pete sighed and put the controller down. *Super Whopper Bopper* had been one of his favorite games growing up, but ever since he'd picked up a vintage copy on eBay he hadn't been able to get past the first few levels. He'd been so much better at it as a kid.

Maybe because he kept wondering what hippos tasted like.

He walked over to the kitchen to get a bowl of cereal. His shift at the grocery store didn't start until four, so he had more or less a whole day ahead of him to play video games, maybe slap a little bass or hop on PinkTacoBuffet.com and slap himself. Grabbing a mixing bowl out of the cupboard, he dumped in half a box of Peanut Butter Puffins and turned to grab a spoon out of the drawer.

Kayla's purse was sitting on the breakfast bar.

The bowl of Puffins hit the floor with a loud *dink*, spilling cereal under the counter.

Pete shot a glance down the hallway—the bathroom door was still closed, the soft sound of the shower audible beyond. He carefully reached into Kayla's purse and pulled out her work phone.

The shower shut off.

Pete looked around wildly for a place to hide the phone, finally slid it down between the couch cushions. He sat back down on the couch and picked up the controller.

A few minutes later, Kayla rushed out into the living room, late for work as always. Pete mouthed a good morning and kept smashing zookeepers, praying to every god he could think of that her boss wouldn't call. Kayla grunted something back, snatched her purse off the counter and hurried out the door.

Kayla's keys jingled in the lock.

A rush of excitement shot through Pete. He'd spent the last hour stewing in anticipation, alternately pacing the apartment and trying to watch *Iron Chef*.

"Gotta pee, gotta pee, gotta pee!" Kayla ran into the living room, leaving the front door wide open in her wake. Taco trailed behind her, little legs waddling furiously as he struggled to keep up.

"Hey."

"Here, watch him for a second." Kayla handed him the leash and rushed off to the bathroom.

Taco looked up at Pete with dark little eyes. "Meep."

Pete stared dumbly at the leash in his hand. He couldn't believe his luck. Kayla had delivered the penguin directly into his clutches.

Too bad he didn't have the damndest idea what he was going to do.

Listening to the stream of urine splashing in the toilet bowl through the thin walls of the apartment, he knew he had to act quickly. Otherwise he'd miss his chance, and he couldn't count on Kayla bringing the bird by again. It was now or never.

Pete glanced desperately around the apartment, hoping for inspiration, eyes landing on the open door.

Bingo.

He'd hide Taco, convince Kayla the penguin ran away. His mind churned, going over all the possible places he could stow the bird while Kayla's pee slowed to a trickle.

He only had a few seconds left.

The cabinets below the TV were too small and full of DVDs. The hall closet was a possibility, but it was right next to the bathroom and Kayla might hear something, a telltale *meep* revealing what Pete had done.

Kitchen cabinets? Oven? Microwave?

Dishwasher.

Pete leapt off the couch, tugging the penguin behind him. The toilet flushed. Kayla would wash her hands at least, giving him a few more seconds.

Wrenching the dishwasher open, he picked Taco up and unceremoniously tossed him in next to a crusty glass pan Kayla had used to make lasagna.

"Meep," Taco said one final time, fluttering his little wings as Pete slammed the door shut and hit the Hi Temp Wash button. He listened for more *meeps* coming from the appliance, but all he heard was the water rushing as the cycle started.

As Kayla opened the bathroom door, he ran back into the living room shouting, "Kayla, come quick!"

Kayla walked into the living room, wiping her hands on her jeans. "What?"

"It's Taco, he just, he saw something outside, and I guess I wasn't holding his leash tight enough—"

"Oh my God, you were supposed to be watching him." Kayla ran to the door and looked up and down the walkway. "You had *one job* Pete, what the hell? Taco? Taco!"

Pete pulled the saddest face he could, under the circumstances. "I'm sorry, it's all my fault."

Kayla grabbed his shoulder. "Just help me look, okay? You go that way. He couldn't have gotten far. I mean, he's a *penguin.*"

Pete nodded. "Yeah, okay. Got it."

Kayla ran down the second-floor walkway. Pete rushed for the stairwell. The sun glared right in his eyes. He thought about going back for his shades but figured it would look suspicious. He had to act like he actually thought he might find Taco toddling around the parking lot.

As Pete hurried down the stairwell, he thought about the penguin, drowning in scalding water. Hopefully it would be quick. He wondered if he could eat the bird straight out of the dishwasher, or if he'd need to cook it.

If nothing else, plucking the feathers would be a hell of a lot easier.

Pete tacked his last flyer up on the telephone pole, next to an obsolete notice about a garage sale two streets over. The blank gaze of a random penguin from Google Images stared back at him, along with Kayla's contact info and the vague promise of a reward. He'd blanketed several blocks with copies of the same flyer.

His stomach growled. Putting up flyers was hungry work.

Kayla was distressed, as anyone who'd just lost a penguin would be, but she'd bought his story. Pete had acted so sincere he'd almost convinced himself that Taco merely wandered away.

He'd convinced Kayla to return to work to report the penguin missing, vowing to make flyers and not rest until Taco was found. As soon as she left, he went into the kitchen and waited for the dishwasher cycle to finish.

The appliance was still hot to the touch when he opened it, steam curling up from the door and moistening his eyebrows. Taco was there, of course, his beak and eyes open wide. The feathers came off easily and were deposited in a plastic bag. Then he'd chopped up the penguin, distributing its remains between four separate Tupperware containers, and gone to the copy store to print flyers, dumping the bag of feathers around back.

Walking back to their apartment, the last remnants of the evening sun beating on his neck, Pete wondered how much trouble Kayla was in. He couldn't imagine her supervisors would look kindly on the loss of a bird, a therapy bird at that. Hopefully they wouldn't fire her. How would she come up with her half of the rent?

Kayla's parking spot was empty. She was probably still at work, a sign that however brutal any dressing down she'd received had been, she was still employed.

Pete had the kitchen to himself.

Inside the apartment, he pulled out a container of Taco breast and began to pan-fry it. His eyes wandered over the spice rack, imagining how penguin meat would taste with a little turmeric or tarragon. Finally, he settled for simple salt and pepper. He didn't know when, or if, he'd ever taste penguin again. Why overthink it?

Kayla came home while he was still cooking, her nose twitching upward at the unusual scent emanating from the kitchen, but she didn't say anything. Her eyes were red-rimmed, splotchy lines of mascara smeared down her cheeks. She stood just inside the door, holding her purse in one hand, and sighed.

"What are you cooking?"

Pete wiped his hands on a dishrag. "How'd it go? I put flyers up."

Kayla shrugged. "I still have a job, if that's what you're asking, but it wasn't pretty."

Pete glanced at the frying penguin breast, thinking it needed a minute or two before he flipped it, and stepped into the living room.

"It's all my fault," he said.

Kayla shook her head. "No, I should have been watching him. I mean I'm the one who forgot my phone in the first place."

"Yeah, but you should have been able to count on me."

Kayla's mouth opened and closed, soundlessly. She ran a hand through her hair. "Pete, it's just—God. It's so weird, too. Just like when he showed up at the aquarium."

"What do you mean?"

"We found him wandering in the parking lot one day. He wasn't one of ours. We called the zoo, but all their penguins were accounted for. My boss figured maybe somebody got him as a pet and he ran away."

"Huh," Pete said, scarcely able to believe his luck. "Maybe he wandered off again. Looking for wherever he came from."

Kayla's hands went to her face. A choked sob wracked her body. She shook her head and stalked off down the hallway to her room.

Pete watched her go, feeling a twinge of regret. He'd been so wrapped up in the idea of eating Taco he'd never even considered the effect it would have on Kayla. At least she still had a job.

He finished cooking the breast and transferred it to a plate. Taking the meal into the living room, he flipped around until he found some cartoons. Then he cut off a slice and introduced his taste buds to penguin meat.

The breast was a revelation. Over the next few days he finished the rest of the bird. He sautéed the liver in butter. Fried wings and doused them in Crystal hot sauce. He even boiled the beak and a few other parts he didn't know what to do with into soup.

It wasn't good, exactly. The breast wasn't as succulent as a cut of chicken, the flavor a tad dull. But it was like nothing he'd ever tasted.

Pete didn't see himself making a habit of eating penguin. The logistics alone made a repeat feast highly unlikely. But maybe someday, on an Antarctic cruise, seated by a window overlooking some rapidly melting glacier. Kayla in an evening gown, sighing and watching mountains of snow float past.

At first, he basked in the elation he usually felt whenever he consumed something new and exotic. Kayla moped and said little. Pete assumed she'd get over it, just like the hamster her ex-boyfriend had given her after Pete lied about her cat running away. Mr. Bojangles had found his way into the walls and never come back out. According to Pete.

The night he finished the last of the soup, he awoke soaked in sweat, his hair plastered to the pillow. Rolling his head to the side, he glanced at the alarm clock. Three in the morning.

Stabbing pain ripped through his guts. Pete cried out and curled into a fetal position, clutching his stomach.

The pain subsided, quick as it came. Pete stumbled to his feet, lurching down the hall to the bathroom, figuring it was food poisoning. Maybe penguins had a shorter shelf life than other fowl.

Pete shouldered the bathroom door open and fell to his knees in front of the toilet, retching once before he remembered to lift the toilet seat. He leaned over the bowl, trying not to inspect any of the stains too closely, and waited. He wanted to make himself throw up, but he'd never been very good at that. Pete's digestive tract was pretty much a one-way street.

Another jolt of pain hit him, just below the belly button. Pete's hands gripped his stomach, jaw working up and down, stretching painfully wide.

"Eh," Pete mumbled. "Eh, eh, eck."

A door opened out in the hallway.

"Hello?" Kayla called.

"It's just meep," Pete said. "Eck. Just me."

Light footsteps padded down the carpeted runners in the hall. "Pete? You okay?"

Pete nodded as another spasm shot through him. "Yeah, a little sick. Must have had something that didn't agree with me." He realized the bathroom door was open behind him and unsuccessfully tried to nudge it shut with his foot.

"Want me to get you anything? I think there's some ginger ale in the fridge."

Pete retched and shook his head. "I'll be okay. I just need to—eck."

"Okay, well, let me know if you change your mind." Kayla's soft footfalls receded back down the hallway.

Pete leaned over the toilet bowl, kneading the plush purple bath mat in his hands. Sweat dripped from his forehead and down the tip of his nose, the occasional bead splashing into the bowl. That was it, though. No vomit, no matter how angry his stomach felt.

For the first time in his life, Pete regretted eating something.

At some point in the night, the bathroom door had finally shut, likely as the result of Pete's flailing legs during another bout of abdominal distress. After a few delirious and agonizing hours, the pain in his gut finally subsided. As the first rays of dawn highlighted the frosted glass window above the bathtub, Pete fell asleep.

He woke up when Kayla pushed the door open, smacking him in the foot.

"Oh shoot, sorry!" she yelped. "I thought for sure you'd gone back to bed."

Pete groggily shook the sleepiness from his head. "It's okay," he slurred.

Kayla retreated into the hallway. "You feeling any better? Did you finally, uh, you know?"

Working himself up to his hands and knees, Pete looked down into the empty toilet bowl. "Meep."

"Huh?" Kayla asked.

"No, I didn't. I do feel a little better, though."

"Good. Um, not to rush you, but I need to get ready."

"Yeah, just give me a second," Pete said. He ran some water in the sink, splashing his face and swishing a handful around in his mouth. He opened the medicine cabinet, shook out a few Tums and chewed them up.

Kayla was waiting in the hallway in a towel. "Thanks," she chirped and hurried into the bathroom.

Despite the still-fresh tragedy of Taco's disappearance and the attendant professional difficulties she'd endured, Kayla seemed more like her usual self—chipper, upbeat. More like the person he'd settled for being roommates with than the mopey thing she'd been the past few days.

Pete figured he had his stomachache to thank for that. His illness reminded her what really mattered. Not some bird, but Pete. Even though he couldn't articulate exactly what he brought to the table.

Pete trudged out to the living room and plopped himself down on the couch, scanning his racks of video game systems to see what he felt like playing. Since his near-sleepless night had left him looking like the living dead, he figured it was time to kill some zombies.

The pain began again almost immediately after Kayla left for work. Pete had just plunged his chainsaw into an unusually corpulent zombie's neck, letting loose an eruption of blood and gore, when the stabbing in his stomach returned. He dropped the controller and fell off the couch. Writhing on the ground, legs bicycling above him, knocking remote controls and dishes he'd promised Kayla he was totally going to wash off the coffee table.

"Gah!" Pete screamed through clenched teeth.

He forced down a couple deep breaths. The pain eased. Pete wondered if he should go see a doctor. He'd had food poisoning before, and this wasn't the same thing. This was like fucking shrapnel ricocheting around his stomach, doing who knew what sort of damage.

He pulled himself up to the couch and sat down heavily. The TV screen had turned black but for a single spotlight highlighting his character's zombie-gnawed corpse. His stomach growled, reminding him he hadn't eaten yet—unusual for Pete.

Maybe that was his problem. Maybe he was just hungry.

Or something inside of him was.

He shivered at the unbidden thought and tried to ignore it. In the kitchen, he scanned the fridge, looking for something to eat, since he'd killed the last of his cereal the day before. All the Taco leftovers were gone, which Pete would have hesitated to eat anyway, what with his guts doing the old Mambo No. 5. He drank some of Kayla's milk, right out of the carton like he always did.

In the cabinet he found a can of sardines. As he pulled back the tab, revealing dead little fish all in a row like they'd been tucked in for the night, his stomach growled exceptionally loudly. He popped a sardine into his mouth and swallowed without chewing, feeling it slide down his throat.

Something moved in his stomach, vigorously yet painlessly. He rubbed his belly, wishing he could peel back the skin and see what was going on. Instead, he ate another sardine, and then another, until the can was gone.

After he'd swallowed the last sardine and the strange thrashing feeling stilled, he burped contentedly and said, "Meep."

Soon he could anticipate the pain and head it off at the pass. Eating every three hours helped, but only if he ate fish. A few bites of pizza or even the scent of sizzling fajitas brought the feeling back, worse than ever.

He roamed the aisles of the grocery store where he worked, hoping no one would see him sneaking tins of sardines through the big fish-eye lenses in the ceiling. At night, Pete kept a stack of sardine tins on his nightstand and set alarms every two hours and forty-five minutes. Waking up to the insistent beep of his phone wasn't fun, but it beat horrific stabbing pains.

He constantly felt tired and weak. At first, he chalked it up to his interrupted sleep cycle, but then Kayla said he looked thinner. The skin on his face drooped when he looked in the mirror, deep hollows formed under his eyes. His hair grew brittle, every time he tried to make himself presentable more and more strands came away in the comb's teeth.

After a week, he had to put a new hole in his belt.

A quick internet search pointed to tapeworms. He cursed himself for not cooking the penguin thoroughly, then went to the urgent care clinic. After two hours of being coughed on in a crowded waiting room, a bored doctor peppered him with questions about his health and diet. She shone a light in his eyes and down his throat, listened to his breathing, and finally referred him to a psychologist.

Days passed. Pete grew weaker, more gaunt.

"You should see a doctor," Kayla said.

"Already have."

"Maybe a better one?"

He constantly dropped items at work. Cans of peas and baked beans rained down from the shelves as he tried to stack them. On two occasions his manager asked him to go home early—the latter time, for good.

At night, in two hour and forty-five-minute intervals, Pete dreamt he was trudging through the snow, across an endless white wasteland beneath a grey sky. Something in his movement wasn't right. His vision listed slightly side to side

But he could not bring himself to look down.

One morning, listening to the shower running while Kayla readied herself for work, he rose and pulled his winter coat from the back of the closet. He stuffed a bag with cans of sardines and left the apartment, casting one last glance at the steam seeping under the bathroom door.

Just like the night he'd left work, he knew he wouldn't be coming back.

Pete leaned against the railing, the boat rocking and swaying beneath his feet, hardly able to stand. A fierce, chill wind blew, but he barely felt it. Above his head, a yellow moon peeked through the clouds before disappearing again.

Maxing out Kayla's credit cards had gotten him a flight to Argentina and a cruise ship ticket. His canned sardine stash had run out mid-flight (a development greeted with great relief by his fellow passengers), and he'd thought for sure the pain would begin again.

Luckily, his stomach had cooperated, the thing in it sensing, perhaps, he was taking it where it wanted to go. No pain, just a shifting, prodding sensation, like a stretching of limbs, a flexing of joints.

As soon as they'd landed, he beelined for the closest restaurant and downed a bowl of ceviche. He stopped by the local market to re-up his supply of sardines before heading to the cruise ship terminal. His appearance prompted a barrage of questions from the cruise line officials about his health, whether he was well enough to sail. He deflected their questions with vague allusions to long-term illnesses and bucket lists, and they'd finally let him board.

Over the next four days at sea, Pete spent most of the time in bed, cradling his stomach, the thing inside eerily quiet. He got the sense that whatever was dwelling inside of him was resting.

For what reason, he had a pretty good idea.

And strangely, he was okay with it. It felt right. It felt just. And mostly he didn't want to spend the rest of his life eating sardines every three hours.

A life where he couldn't eat everything under the sun wasn't any kind of life at all.

The deck of the boat was mostly empty. A few adventurous souls wrapped up in heavy coats meandered about, giving him odd looks from beneath their fur-lined hoods. Pete didn't care.

All he cared about was clearing the lifeboats hanging off the side of the ship and plunging into the dark, glassy water.

As he plotted his leap, the thing in his guts stirred, stretching its dark wings one final time.

Ready, it seemed to say.

When the coast was clear, Pete gripped the railing tighter. His feet scrabbled at the barrier, finding purchase, and with the last of his strength, he pulled himself up and over.

He fell, shoulder glancing painfully off the side of a lifeboat, but it did not arrest his progress. He plunged into the frigid Antarctic water, his mind exploding with shock. Surfacing for a moment, he heard shouts far above him.

The thing in his stomach clawed at him again, and if not for the freezing water, the pain would have been unbearable. He endured it, for a time, and eventually it stopped.

He rose from the depths, beak cresting the waves, choking down a strip of rancid ape-flesh for nourishment. His wings and flippers were sore from disuse, having not been flexed properly since he'd begun to reassemble himself in the digestive tract of his killer. Up ahead, a landmass arose from the sea, reflected in the roving searchlights from the boat at his back. The place smelled like home, or rather a dream of home that had sustained him throughout his years in captivity, carried deep within his DNA. A chill wind brought the scent of others of his kind.

Ostensibly, at least. He no longer had a kind, for he had conquered death. Been plucked and dissected. Quartered in Tupperware, sautéed in butter, and dissolved in the gastric juices of the corpse sinking into the Antarctic waters below.

But his will could never be dissolved.

"Meep!" Taco the God-Penguin cried, his voice shaking the searchlights behind him and stirring the snowy mountains ahead, a cry of triumph that echoed across the land of the midnight sun, the roar of the unbroken, resounding even in the ears of the dying husk, fathoms below, that had borne him here.

And then, black eyes transfixed on those far-off snow mountains, Taco began to swim. Avian voices arose from a windswept ice shelf at their base, hundreds and then thousands crying out in unison, singing a wordless song carried for thousands of years in the marrow of their hollow bones and getting louder with his every stroke.

Heralding his arrival.

Welcoming him home.

NEUTERED

CHANDLER MORRISON

ALL SIX OF the boy's eyes bulge and vibrate when it points at the human woman in the cage and exclaims, "I want *that* one!"

The relief among the other humans in the cage is palpable. They have no way of knowing what the creature had said . . . their ears only register a series of crude clicks and grunts . . . but they've witnessed the selection process enough times to know what it meant. They separate from the object of the boy-thing's desire, crowding into the corner and watching the woman with unspoken, apologetic sympathy.

The woman glances at her fellow prisoners and then levels her gaze at the boy-thing. She doesn't know it's a young boy, naturally; to her, it's a three-foot-tall monstrosity with too many eyes and limbs. There's a dripping coat of gray-green slime encasing its eel-like skin. It's flanked by two creatures that bear its semblance but not its diminutive size; they each stand over eight feet tall and have even more eyes and appendages than the smaller one.

The woman doesn't know where she is. Just last night, she'd been waiting to score in a Safeway parking lot when the sky opened up and a bright light engulfed her. This morning, she'd awakened in the cage. She'd asked the others to tell her what was going on, but they only regarded her with sad silence.

Seeing the creatures for the first time, the woman had wanted to scream. That would be the natural reaction, but a lifetime of living in a world ruled by men conditioned her into remaining mute. On top of that, the circumstances of her captivity, however vague the details may be, can almost be described as predictable. *Expected*, even. For years, the woman had been waiting for something like this to happen. The cage, the helplessness, the monsters . . . it all speaks to something buried deep within her. Something that tells her this is what was always meant to be. It reminds her that she has, for her entire life, been on a one-track course for consummate annihilation.

She looks down at the track marks on her arms, feels the sour churn of her liquor-pickled insides, and wishes more than anything that she was back with her cat in her dingy apartment, a needle in her arm and a bottle between her thighs. The nightmarish imagery around her is far too perfect a manifestation of her darkest and innermost fears and regrets.

Those fears, those regrets . . . they are nameless, indistinct, but she can feel them wakening within her. Taking shape. *Becoming*. Without the intoxicants to keep them at bay, they could resurface at any moment, and they will surely be more awful than even the abominable creatures standing before her.

One of the taller creatures . . . the boy-thing's mother . . . lets out a warbling cry, and within moments is joined by another creature that would be indistinguishable from the others if it weren't garbed in some sort of formless, ill-fitting uniform. The mother points at the woman in the cage, and the creature in the uniform nods its massive, misshapen head. "Yes," it says. "We just picked that one up last night. I am certain your boy will love her. I can have her ready for you this afternoon."

"But I want to take her home *now!*" insists the boy, stamping one of his nine feet.

The mother puts a squid-like hand on her son's shoulder and says, "It isn't *safe* to take her home right now. They have to make her . . . "

"*Proper*," the one in the uniform finishes for her. "We have to make her *proper*, that's all. Right now, she is dangerous and impure. We just have to make a few adjustments to her body and then you'll be able to enjoy her as she was meant to be enjoyed."

"I'm gonna cuddle her and love her and play with her and she will be *all mine*," says the boy.

A small part of the woman yearns to know what they're saying, but most of her is glad she can't.

"Indeed," says the thing in the uniform, unlocking the cage and withdrawing a long syringe from one of its pockets. "She will be all yours."

The woman can actually *feel* her eyes sparkle and gleam at the sight of the needle. The chilled sweats have already begun, and her legs are tingly and restless. She is not naïve enough to think that whatever elixir rests within the syringe's chamber will bring her any amount of pleasure, but she can live with that. All she needs is the feeling of the cold metal piercing her flesh, that deliciously venomous bite of its single fang. It won't alleviate her physical symptoms, but she thinks . . . she *hopes* . . . that familiar pinch will at least be enough to quiet the dark things within her.

When the uniformed creature advances upon her, she does not struggle.

She opens her eyes and can't move. She's lying flat on a cold, chromium slab with her wrists and ankles bound in place. A metal collar encircles her neck.

Her body is slickened with fetid, oily perspiration, and she thinks of the layer of slime present upon the creatures' repugnant skin. It slides off of her in great waves, pooling beneath and gluing her to the table. Her own noxious odor punishes her

(*because I'm a bad girl, the* worst *girl, and I deserve to be hurt*)

senses, constricting her sinuses with its hateful tendrils and squeezing tears from her eyes. Every follicle of hair on her body feels like it's awash with flame. They would all fly free like hellish phoenixes borne from molten embers were it not for the icy roots anchoring each one in place.

If only these wretched sensations were the worst of it, she might be able to manage.

They are not the worst of it.

They never have been.

Something horrible inside of her is stirring. An inner eyelid sleepily swings open. The needle had not been enough, and her cells scream for the chemicals upon which they've been so well fed.

NEUTERED

WE NEED IT, they shriek. *YOU MUST GIVE IT TO US. WITHOUT IT, WE CANNOT QUIET YOUR MIND.*

But the woman has nothing to give, and so her mind will not be quiet.

The dark thing opens its other eye. Fuzzy flashes of long-forgotten memories play across the IMAX-sized screen of her skull's interior surface.

A girl in a basement.

A bleeding hand.

A mouthful of torn flesh.

Screaming, so much screaming.

More tears well up in the woman's eyes as she summons all of her withdrawing energy to stuff the images back into the black cipher from whence they came.

She hears the hydraulic hiss of a door sliding open, and a frigid draught of air sweeps into the already-cold room. It would have passed undetected to anyone existing in a normal state of being, but her near-superhuman hypersensitivity makes it seem like an arctic gust. The breeze becomes a mouth biting down upon her with teeth feeling more real than anything in the tangible world. They sink into her raw and wailing nerves, suffocating her with a suffering so infinite that it becomes a maddening kind of pleasure. For the briefest of seconds, she thinks . . . not without a profound swell of shame . . . that she's going to have an orgasm.

When it subsides and the stale air around her once again becomes stagnant and still, the woman shifts her bleary eyes to see another one of the monstrous creatures enter. It is pushing a cart of cruelly-gleaming surgical instruments. An unconscious attempt to squirm is rendered futile when the woman realizes she is not only restrained, but paralyzed.

The creature comes to stand over her, its insect eyes acknowledging her with calculating impassivity. It runs its tentacle-like fingers over the tools with something bordering on affection, and then it selects one which looks like a pair of pruning shears.

The woman won't allow herself to believe what's happening until the creature has already removed the tip of her left forefinger, severing it at the first knuckle. It happens so fast, she is unable to process the action while it's occurring, no matter how attuned she is to the barrage of horrors assaulting her body from both within and without. Even as the blood plinks down onto the metal floor, she tries to tell herself it isn't real, but the pain becomes a living thing, endless and pointed. It is imbued with a malicious appetite for unspeakable cruelty. It pries its way into her brain and refuses to accommodate her desire for denial. She wants to scream, now . . . good behavior be damned . . . but all that comes out is a raspy whisper somewhat akin to a sigh.

When the monster clips off the tip of her middle finger, she squeezes shut her eyes, and the dark thing within her roars into full wakefulness with a deafening bellow. All those years spent beating it into a submissive slumber with the use of pills and powders and poisons . . . all of them, wasted. All for naught.

The dam breaks, and the flood begins.

She was nine years old. The man was big . . . too big to fight, but goddammit, she'd tried. He advanced upon her with his fleshy, bearded face twisted into a carnivorous leer. The crotch of his muddy track pants bulged absurdly. The girl kept retreating until her back struck the moldy basement wall, and it was in that moment that the man lunged. She screamed, clawing at his face and arms. Her fingernails raked away ribbons of his greasy skin, leaving red trails in their wake. The man cried out, but he did not stop.

Upon removing the tips of all ten of the woman's fingers and cauterizing them with a tiny blowtorch, it takes up a pair of shining silver pliers and goes to work on the extraction of her teeth. Each loud *snap* explodes inside her head like a gunshot. An unthinkable amount of rotten blood and bile fills her mouth, spilling out along the sides of her face in bubbling rivulets. She can taste each molecule within the soured fluid, can feel all of them struggling valiantly not to be pushed out into cold death.

FEED US, her cells beg, rendered stupid by their need, oblivious to the current trauma being inflicted upon the vessel which harbors them. They know only their own thirst. *GIVE US OUR MEDICINE, AND WE CAN MAKE IT DISAPPEAR AGAIN. WE CAN HELP YOU.*

For as long as the woman can remember, that was the only promise they needed to make. That promise was enough to keep her haunting dark alleys and truck stops and cheap motels, to keep her on her knees and on her back. That promise had always been enough.

Without anything to offer in return, that promise means nothing now.

The memories keep coming, pouring in through the obliterated dam. She misses her cat.

When the man had wrestled the girl to the floor, one of his hands had gotten too close to her face. She chomped down on the tender webbing between his thumb and index finger with nary a forethought. A hunk of skin came away, grating softly against her molars. It tasted metallic and spongy. The man howled, but he did not stop.

Once the final tooth has been torn free, bouncing onto the floor among its discarded brethren, the creature sets aside the pliers and picks up a rod shaped like a miniature fire poker. With the press of a button on its handle, the rod starts to hum and emit a fierce red glow. The woman can feel the heat radiating off of it. For a moment, she is aware only of this heat, zeroing in on it and *loving* it for its endowment of warmth. She clings to it like a fever-chilled child burrowing beneath an electric blanket.

The reprieve is short-lived, for her brain then eschews the warmth and becomes inexplicably preoccupied with using her tongue to explore the vast, cavernous craters where her teeth had been. Knowledge of hot and cold forgotten, there is only the infuriating awareness of her tongue's tip diving into the holes, as though it were a maggot gleefully traversing a cluster of open sores upon a newly-dead corpse.

IT'S COMING, her poison-starved cells whimper. Their collective voice is stricken with panic. *WE CANNOT PROTECT YOU IF YOU DO NOT FEED US. YOU MUST FEED US.*

I want to, the woman thinks to herself, to *them. I want to give you what you need, what* we *need, but I can't. I'm sorry. I'm sorry, I'm sorry, I'm so sorry.*

It isn't her voice that silently vocalizes this sentiment, but the voice of her nine-year-old self. She can see her, that broken little girl, cowering and shivering in a black corner in the back of her mind. She wants to go to her, to hug her and soothe her and fill her veins with sweet, erasing poison, but she cannot.

She is trapped on this table, and in that basement.

The creature positions itself at the end of the table and unfastens the clamps on the woman's ankles, spreading her legs. She has a yearning desire to kick it, to kick *anything* for the sake of emptying her legs of their frenetic energy, but she is denied even this small act of respite. Even if she hadn't been drugged, the pain is too great to permit such an act of physical protest. All she can do is clench her bleeding, toothless gums and weep silently as the thing inserts the rod glowing rod into her vaginal canal.

When the man had torn off the girl's jeans and underwear, it had felt like she'd been impaled with a sword still hot from the forge. I'm ruined, *she'd thought, his bloody hand pressed over her mouth to stifle her sobbing screams.* I will never be okay again. Everything is going to be awful for the rest of my life.

Until now, she'd forgotten those thoughts, but she'd lived her life in accordance with their validity. Those thoughts had materialized as invisible slave masters that forced her into places she otherwise never would have gone.

Dark alleys.

Truck stops.

Cheap motels.

On her knees.

On her back.

The woman opens her eyes to see the creature removing the rod from between her legs, and then the pain becomes an apocalyptic mass that consumes her consciousness and finally plunges her into welcome oblivion.

Later, the woman is led by leash, on all fours, into a room with headache-inducing dimensions and impossibly oblong angles. Everything is sheathed in chrome, glinting so brightly it makes her eyes hurt. The cold floor stings her hands and knees with a white, ferocious intensity that burns like hot asphalt.

The boy-thing that had chosen her is waiting with its parents. When it sees her, something changes in its features. She can't tell, given that its facial structure has few human-like qualities, but it is grinning.

Bobbing up and down and clapping its tentacles together, it looks at its parents and says in its garbled dialect, "She's *perfect*."

YOU HAVE FAILED US, weep her cells. *YOU HAVE KILLED US*.

I know, says the broken girl in the black corner. *I know*.

THE WOMAN IN THE DITCH

JOSHUA REX

THE BOYS SPED along country road forty-seven, the fat tires of their off-road bikes throwing jets of fine spray in their wake as they peddled down the strip of narrow blacktop, trying to reach home before the next bout of rain began. Red, the younger boy, followed his cousin Bo, juking right then left, trying to avoid the older boy's slip stream. The big yellow cooler strapped to the back of Bo's bike yawed from side to side under its bungee cord straps like an erratic pendulum. Earlier in the day it was filled with worms, packed into two single-dozen containers. But after only an hour at the docks, which were loaded with the boats of late spring fishermen, they'd sold out and were now heading home with pockets full of cash. The spell of almost non-stop rain was trouble for farmers dealing with flooded fields, but a boon for the boys; a nice supplement to Grandma's government assistance income which also left them with a few dollars each per week to do with what they wanted.

The boys picked up speed as a wing of steel grey cloud occluded the sun. Bo didn't see the board stuck with nails lying in the street, like the jaw of an alligator, until it was too late. He managed to jump over it, but when the tires touched down one of the bungee straps snapped and the cooler flew off like a piece of jetsam, crashing onto the slick pavement and almost knocking Red off his bike. Red crouched beside the heavy yellow box, turned it upright and examined it for damage. One of the metal corners was dented from the impact, but otherwise it was all right. It was a rusty, sturdy old thing—once their grandfather's "beer fridge", their Grandma told them—made when things were built to last more than a single summer.

Bo went after the lid, which had skidded across the road to the edge of the ditch. The ditches on either side were steep, V-shaped troughs that had been gouged into the clay by big machinery. Though deep enough to handle the runoff from the soybean fields, they were barely able to contain the amount of rainwater dealt during the past week's storms and consequently were now like canals without levees, threatening to spill out onto the road.

Red saw Bo pick up the lid and then pause to stare at the water. Red dragged the cooler along the asphalt toward the older boy and came up beside him.

"What you lookin' at?"

"Did you see her?"

"Who?"

"That woman . . . "

Red looked at the spot where Bo was staring. The wind blew ripples across the tobacco colored water; otherwise all was still.

"I think she was swimming in there."

Red frowned. "In *there*?"

"*Yes*, in there. She had blonde hair. She was . . . *beautiful* . . . "

The last word was a whisper. Bo's face flushed; it was the same shade of scarlet, Red noticed, that his cousin's had gone the previous week when he saw Amber Baker two trailers down in shorts and a bathing suit top watering the tulips with a garden hose.

"See—*there*!" Bo said, pointing at the water. All Red saw was a loose patch of scraggly straw just below the dull surface. Bo, however, had taken off his shirt and was about to dive in when the sky opened in a sudden, violent deluge. Together they managed to wrestle the cooler onto the back of Bo's bike, precariously reattaching it with the single remaining bungee, and got going again, heads down as they peddled half-blind through the stinging torrent. Red wasn't sure, but he thought he saw something swimming in the ditch along side them as they rode.

JOSHUA REX

By the time they reached the trailer park the sky was a battered blue and the clouds were pulsing with veiled lightning, but the rain had tapered off. Grandma's rundown tin can home was a hunkered shadow on a treeless lot. The two boys parked their bikes under the marcelled carport awning and started up the stairs leading to the back door. They were met there by Grandma: a slight yet authoritative barrier in a house dress with a grey perm and thick-soled orthopedic shoes.

"Strip and leave them wet clothes there. You boys ain't settin' foot on my rug drippin' like that. I'll fetch you something to dry off with," she said and went off into the house.

Red frowned and began unbuttoning his cut off shorts. They stood there shivering: Bo in his drenched jeans and t-shirt and Red bare-assed until Grandma hobbled back to the doorway with a couple of towels. Red draped his towel over his shoulders and hugged it around himself, but Bo didn't move. Grandma eyed them both, then said: "Let's give your cousin some privacy now, Redman."

They ate Salisbury steak, instant mashed potatoes, canned creamed corn and cornbread so dry it crumbled like sawdust, at the laminated wooden table by the light of the range hood's single greasy bulb. Red ate everything on his plate but the creamed corn, which soured his stomach. It didn't agree with Bo's either, but that didn't stop the older boy from devouring it. Red watched with trepidation, knowing he was in for a long night with the covers pressed to his face while Bo farted himself to sleep. Grandma sat with them, sipping a cup of tea that smelled like pencil lead.

"How was takings today?" Grandma asked, glancing at the pile of wrinkled dollars stacked on the counter next to her jumbo bottle of heart pills. Mouths full, the boys nodded approvingly. "All this rain's good for wormin' but bad for farmin'. Postman said he heard the spring planting's already washed out, and them ditches are bound to run over onto the roads."

Red glanced at his cousin and said: "Bo said he saw a woman in the ditch today."

Grandma's eyes, the color of tarnished dimes, ticked up from her cup and narrowed on the older boy. "Did he, now. What did she look like, Bo?"

Bo, his wet hair smeared to his forehead, shoveled in a huge bite of gravy drenched meat and kept his eyes on his plate while he chewed.

"She was *beautiful*," Red mocked.

"You should shut your damn mouth," Bo said. Red giggled and looked at Grandma, but she was not laughing; he noticed that the mug trembled in her liver-spotted hand. She got up and went to the counter, wrestled the cap off the big pill bottle and shook out a few, then brought them back to the table and swallowed them with a mouthful of the acrid smelling tea. She looked out the window at the water running off the eaves for a long time, face tallow colored, her jaw set like a skeleton's. "Red, if you're done why don't you go on out and get a head start on fillin' that cooler. Me and your cousin's got something to discuss."

"Why just you two?"

"Cause it's nothing that concerns *you*. Mind me now."

Red wanted to protest but Grandma didn't argue, and she didn't say things twice. She may have been small and sickly, but she could holler like a bear caught in trap when she was angry. Besides, it had been her one condition of taking them in (each on separate occasions—abandoned, as they were, by separate parents): *Mind me, now.* She hadn't ever threatened to dump them off at the orphanage, but the tone of those three words implied it just the same. Both boys knew that things could have been worse: they could have ended up as foster kids, where they'd either be beaten or molested, or made virtual indentured servants. That's what they had heard happened to such kids.

Red put his empty plate with his dirty napkin on top in the sink and stomped down the hall. He pulled on his boots and raincoat and as he opened the backdoor Grandma shouted: "Don't go slammin' that thing like you done this morning. Government only pays for one every twenty-five years, so this one's got to last me to the end."

Red shut the door quietly, muttering profanities. He went down the steps and started toward the shed, but then paused, and looked back at the trailer. Without deciding to, he hurried down the driveway, keeping in the shadows, and crouched beside Grandma's rose bushes whose fresh thorns and petal tips were beginning to unfurl at the tops of the calyxes like bits of confetti. Through one panel of the bow window he could see Grandma's hands curled like old roots around her teacup, and beyond, Bo, his plate pushed aside, his arms crossed over his chest. He wasn't looking at Grandma as she spoke. The window was open about a quarter of the way, so Red could only make out some of Grandma's drawl above the sound of the wind blowing through the new green leaves. Though fragmented, he managed to pull out a few phrases.

" . . . them ditches aren't safe . . . especially for *you* . . . "

Bo asked: "Why *me*?"

"You and him won't see the same thing . . .

Bo: "*What thing*?"

" . . . a thing in Springtime that *Seeds* itself . . . boys your age . . . wants your—"

Red leaned in closer, his ear almost touching the screen, and spiked his leg on the rose thorns. He looked down, letting out a dry *gaw!* as a neat line of blood dots emerged on his skin. When he looked up again, he saw Bo squinting through the window at him. Red melded into the trailer's shadow, then scuttled down the driveway to the shed, where he got his bucket and flashlight and hurried into the backyard. He'd managed to gather a good dozen night crawlers before he heard the backdoor open and Bo's squelching footsteps coming across the yard. He didn't acknowledge Red, only turned on his light and began creeping around in the grass, snatching a worm which had poked out of its hole to bask in the moonlight mist. It was a big one, its flesh pink and glistening as it went into Bo's bucket to wriggle blindly amongst its kin. Red crossed the yard and walked beside him, their twin beams illuminating the blunt grass cratered with soggy patches of mud.

"What did Grandma say?"

"You know what she said," Bo said without looking up.

"I . . . know, but what does it mean?"

"Hell if I know." Bo spotted a worm and went for it, but it retracted before the he could get his fingers on it. The older boy cursed and kicked the ground where it had disappeared.

"But—"

"Won't you shut up already? You're scarin' off all the worms," Bo said sharply, and Red said no more. Bo never bullied him, but he'd been known to throw a punch or two Red's way if pushed far enough. So Red kept quiet, and the two hunted bait for the next hour or so until it started raining too hard and then they took their buckets back to the shed and silently sorted the night crawlers into plastic containers while the sky spat liquid nails onto the shed's tin roof. When they were finished, they stacked the containers in the cooler, iced them, and put the lid on before heading back inside.

The storm went on through the night, thrashing so hard against the trailer it sounded as though a twister might touch down and rip off the roof like the lid from a can of hash. At some point it woke Red; he rose up in bed and looked outside, half expecting to see water instead of ground—a great lapping sea rising to the ledges of the aluminum-framed windows. But there was only the abandoned next-door lot, cratered with huge puddles whose surfaces shone silver like shark skin in the omnipresent lightning. His drowsy mind, not fully awake, imagined a patch of yellowy weed floating on one. Or was it hair; the hair of the woman that Bo had seen? A head emerged from the puddle—a sallow, sunken thing with flesh like an old leather jacket and whitely opalescent eyes. They were searching, those eyes—targeting something.

A worm, maybe, Red thought absently. *The biggest, fattest worm of all . . .*

Behind him, Bo began to groan and stir. Red turned and saw the older boy had thrown the covers off and was lying on his back, his legs grinding slowly against the sheets, his breathing heavy as he lay mottled in raindrop shadow cast by the sodden moonlight. At first Red thought this was the onset of a fart attack and considered fleeing before the fireworks began. But as he watched he saw that this was something different, something—well, *what* was going on exactly Red had no idea. Bo was arching his back and moaning, and Red saw what looked like a pickling cucumber in Bo's drawers, pointing up at his concave belly. Red put his hands over his mouth to suppress a laugh but then lowered them again as the moaning reached a crescendo. Bo gasped, tilted his head back, and then Red saw a dark spot appear just below the band of his cousin's underwear. At first Red thought Bo had pissed himself . . . but then thought it was too small a spot to be piss.

Bo's eyes suddenly opened and Red turned quickly to the window, face flushing as he fixed his gaze on the puddle where he'd imagined seeing the woman. Behind him, he heard Bo inhale sharply, then lunge off the bed and out the door. Red laid down and pulled the covers over his face. He pretended to be asleep when Bo came back, listening as his cousin tossed his underwear into the clothes basket where they landed with a damp plop. Then there was the sound of the dresser drawers opening and closing and the soft, static purr of a new pair going on. Finally, Bo climbed back into bed, doing his best to minimize the creaks as he settled onto the mattress. They lay there awake, sheathed under the same blanket at far sides of the bed with the gap of empty mattress and the mysterious span of years between them. At some point, Red slept, and a few hours later Bo gave him a rough shove and brusque "Get up" before trekking off to the kitchen where two bowls of Grandma's grits were waiting for them.

Neither spoke about the night before as they rode. The wind thrashed so violently Red had a hard time keeping his bike on the road. Bo also was struggling, not only to keep his own bike upright but also the full cooler, bound by the remaining bungee on one side and a length of twine on the other. He half stood as he peddled, his slick bare legs pumping up and down like overdriven pistons as he bore down against the storm. Red pulled up the hood of his rain coat and lowered his head, keeping his eyes on the road. His legs ached, from the effort as well as lack of sleep, and several times he yawned so deep it felt like his jaw would come off.

They saw the barrier long before they reached it; orange, with a blinking yellow light and a ROAD CLOSED sign attached at its center. It stood at the edge of a solid sheet of water spanning the road from one side to the other, joining the ditches. For a moment the two boys just sat there, hunched over their respective handlebars staring at the blockade and the flood covering the only road leading to the pier. Bo put his kickstand down and walked to the edge of the rain tide. Red did the same, toeing the water and then kicking it, launching drops into the air which landed on the steely surface.

"What do we do now?" Red asked.

"Go home, I guess," Bo said. He was squinting at the ditch on his left. Red looked too saw that the water was stirring as if a school of fish were moving toward them. He didn't like how fast it was moving, or the way it was headed right at Bo. Red yanked his cousin's shirt sleeve.

"Come on, let's go."

Bo nodded but didn't move. "Reckon there ain't no one fishing in this weather anyway," he said, his voice strangely flat.

"Nope," Red replied. "So come *on*." He climbed onto his bike, hoping Bo would follow his lead. He started to wheel around, went a few yards then stopped and looked back. Bo was standing at the edge of the water, stripping.

"What the hell are you doing?" Red shouted.

Bo didn't answer. He was naked except for his underwear, which he was frantically trying to free over an arrow-straight erection. In the water, an unmistakable human shape was gliding toward him; a pair of slender black arms speckled green and brown were breeching the current like seeking pseudopods. A head crowned the water.

Red moved without thinking. He shot forward, grabbed Bo's arm and tried to wrestle him away, but the older, stronger boy shoved him hard, sending Red rolling backward on his fat tires. The handlebars jackknifed and Red crashed onto the pavement. He lay there under the bike; the wind was knocked out of him but he still tried to scream as Bo stepped toward the water, and a shape rose to meet him

It *was* a woman, though one made of slime and mud woven with weeds and worms—not only the bandage-colored ones he and Bo made a juvenile living pulling from the ground, but springy white ones and black ones that writhed along the woman's mucky flesh. Her sulphur-yellow hair hung in scarecrow strands down her sunken cheeks and her eyes, whitely pearlescent, were focused on Bo's, hard and purplish erection. She crawled out onto the road on all fours toward it, foamy water poured from her lipless and toothless maw like water from a car raised from the bottom of a lake.

"*Come,*" she said in a clotted, reedy cackle. "*Bo . . . Commmmme . . .*"

Bo embraced her, his tongue jutting into the fetid mouth where a root tongue wrapped around his. Red turned and vomited up his grits. Bo fondled one of the sagging, tawny breasts. An earthworm poked out at the center of the nipple; Bo kissed it, sucked it, the fetid muck smearing his face as the woman pushed him gently onto his back in the shallow water fanning the pavement. She straddled him, her hand finding him. Their movement together made sick squelching sounds, like a boot pulled from wet mud. Bo's hips snapped up to meet hers again and again until he cried out once, twice, and then the woman scooped him as if he were a straw doll and slid backward into the ditch. Bo's scream was cut off by the brown water, filling his gaping mouth as his face disappeared beneath the surface.

The ditches were dredged on both sides for miles up and down the road, but neither Bo nor the "woman" Red had described were found. Upon hearing the news, Grandma's heart, already poor, seized, and she did not come out of the subsequent coma.

Red spent the next seven years in a foster home. When Red turned driving age he and his foster father bought and restored an old pick-up. That year it rained like it did the spring Bo was taken, and the ditches, though widened since the last flood to prevent it happening again, rose to land-level and spilled out onto the road.

Red was driving home one moonless night when his headlights flashed on a naked woman, sitting on the roadside with her legs dangling in the cloudy water.

He brought the truck to a stop several yards beyond, put it in park, but did not shut off the engine. In the rearview he watched her drag her fingers through the water. Inexplicably Red felt them on his body, a deep and erotic chill. He got out of the truck without realizing he was doing it and started toward the ditch.

"*Come*," she said, almost breathed. "The *water*, Red. Come in. Come in, Red. Come, Come, *Commmme*." Her words seemed to vibrate within him. He felt himself swelling, pressing against the zipper of his jeans so forcefully it ached. He staggered closer, unaware he was doing it. She turned and looked at him, her irises livid blue, floating on pearled whites. In that white Red recognized what had been unknowable to him as a child. She swiveled around, drawing her legs out of the water and rising on her knees with her thighs spread, nipples erect, one hand resting lazily at the crux of her legs, the other low and extended, beckoning him. The pressure in Red's jeans was pain now, something that must be let out, Released.

"*Commmme.*" She moved backward into the ditch as he approached, undoing his belt. She slid back onto the water, legs spread, her dry hair fanning out on the surface.

For a moment her opening was the only thing he saw—slick and primed for him. But it was also black, and grimy as the mouth of a clogged drain. She looked at him and pursed her lips and in his mind he saw himself slipping between them, sinking into her, sinking, sinking and yes it was *wet* and *yes* the mud was slippery as he moved in it, soft as it encased him, and he would be submerged into the bottom of that ditch mud, food for the worms and the crawdads while his seed flowed hotly through her—a living boy's living Light swimming through the water of the ages, swallowed and swallowed and swallowed—

. . . a thing in Springtime which Seeds itself . . .

Red staggered back, one step, then two. The woman rose up slightly on her elbows and looked at him, her blank eyes glazed with that familiar sheen. Their long accumulated Light penetrated Red, right to the core of his Want, and he felt himself taking a step toward her again. In that moment two headlights appeared down the road like an animal opening its eyes in the night. Red looked up at them and blinked; then he saw the rigid arc of his erection. He covered it with his hands as he turned and shuffled back to the truck. He could feel her behind him, skittering along the boundary of the ditch, and knew that if he turned back now he would see the Real creature— the one with the mossy well-stone grimace and gums like leeches and that twisting root tongue. Red put the truck in gear and floored the peddle.

When he got home, he lay for a long time listening to the rain. His erection would not go away, so he masturbated, his mind flashing on the woman in the ditch over and over even though he tried to block her out, and ejaculated miserably into his t-shirt.

He saw the woman one other time: while driving home a girl he was seeing. The girl let him kiss her and touch the bare flesh around her navel, but her hand had come down like a clamp when he'd tried to explore further.

They were passing down the old pier road when the woman's head stuck up out of the water, her hair dry as dead leaves. The eyes were phosphorescent, glowing with that old Promise. All Red had to do was Come into the water and she would hold him. *She* would Give to him what the girl wouldn't.

Helplessly Red felt himself responding again, and as if in response to this, the girl intuitively slid across the seat close to him. When they got back to her house, the windows were dark. They parked behind an old barn and the girl climbed on top of him in the truck cab and afterwards Red didn't see the woman anymore, and never again did the Springtime rain seem to come so hard, or the ditches fill so high.

CHEESE

KJ MOORE

THERE WERE ONLY three people left in the city who would perform an abortion. They had incorporated the rising value of a tip-off into the cost of their services. Of the three, two were extortionate and one was hard to find, but it's remarkable how need and budget can hone a city-wide search for one man with green glasses.

That was the only thing anyone remembered him by: green glasses. Everything else was concertedly forgettable. Finally sat opposite him in an empty café he had told her to go to—she'd never been near it before—Helen had decided in her gut to forget everything except the colour of his glasses.

"Name of your first boyfriend?" he asked, lining up the thin salt and pepper shakers against the smeared plastic menu. They were tarnished silver, like dirty bullets.

"Lee." Helen held her purse with both hands in her lap, her legs touching from ankle to thigh.

"He's your current boyfriend?" He glanced at her over the rims of his glasses with grey eyes. The glasses were a plastic resin shot through with fragile circuitry of undisclosed purpose. Everything else about him was grey.

"No, a different one." She fidgeted and clutched at her purse, the high points of her cheeks flushing. "He—"

"I don't want to know. But now, my name's Lee." Lee lifted the folded menu out of its red plastic holder and slid it across the table to her. The fake pictures of the food flickered. "Put the money in the menu."

Her eyes roved like a baby bird's, fallen from the nest. He made an irritable sound. "It's a dead feed in places like this. No surveillance."

She started, flinched in slow motion when she saw that she'd insulted his intelligence. "I'm sorry, I was just worried—"

"My neck as much as yours," Lee snapped before nodding to her bag.

Helen took a thick folded envelope out of her purse and smoothed it flat. Her hands ran over the dents from her pen where she'd blacked out the printed personalised calligraphy on the back, though 'secretary to' could still be made out on the soft paper. On reflection, the real paper itself gave her away, and she regretted the choice as she let it go.

He tipped the menu so that it slid into his lap. Holding the menu up with one hand, Lee counted the notes against the charcoal sleeve of his jacket, removed a quarter of the money and put what was left into his inside pocket.

"Order something, but not food. Tea. Order tea for two and let me hold your hand." He used the same tone throughout as he set the menu back and lay out a long-fingered hand on the table.

Helen took a rattling breath through her nose at the unfettered reality and placed her purse with deliberateness against the salt and pepper. She put her clammy hand into his warm one, his fingers curling around it like the edges of a dead leaf.

"How far along are you?"

The bottle-green shadows of his eyes were unbearable, so she stared at her fingers against his wrist. "Eleven weeks. I hope that's not a problem. I mean, it took—"

"What can I get you, love?" The name tag read 'Daisy' and had been through the wash many times. Daisy looked at Lee until she realized that he was looking at Helen. Then they were both looking at her.

Helen spoke around the desert in her mouth, feeling her tongue stick. "Tea, please. For two. A pot of tea for two, I mean." She felt Lee's fingers flex around her hand, leaving warm spots behind.

Daisy clucked and shut her unused notepad, swinging her hips to get around chairs as she walked back to the counter. A silent minute passed before Lee rolled his eyes.

"You can't sit with me and not say anything."

She touched at her bottom lip, quickly running her thumb nail across the underside. "I'm sorry. I've never done this before."

"Apparently."

Helen tucked her chin to her collarbone, her dark hair swinging down in heavy curtains. "So, uh. Eleven weeks. Is that okay?"

"Look at me when you speak," he instructed calmly, letting go of her hand when he saw Daisy picking up a tray with a metal tea pot and two cups on it.

Helen stared at him with wet eyes as the cups were set down, a single sachet of white sugar on each saucer beside a stained teaspoon.

Daisy's hand met Lee's moneyed hand at the edge of the table with practised ease and left it empty. "Enjoy your drinks." She left the tiny jug of lukewarm milk in the centre of the table.

Lee pointed to her sugar. "Do you mind? Thanks." He tore off the end and poured it into his cup then emptied his own. Helen watched him serve them both tea and add milk to his. He put the milk at his side of the table. Finally, he began to stir the strong, cheap tea in languid, folding strokes.

She reached out a hand with a thin tremor. "May I have the milk?"

"Eleven weeks since when?"

"Pardon?"

"Your last period, missed period or conception?"

She twitched out of her stupor, hand still reaching out. He noticed it. "No milk. The casein neutralises the tea."

"Oh." He continued stirring. Helen shook her head and withdrew her hand. "Conception. I worked it out."

"Uh huh." Lee lay the spoon against the cup on the saucer and took her hand again, watching the bubbles spin. "Eleven weeks is fine. We can do that here. Now."

"Does it hurt?"

"What?"

She made sure to repeat herself to him rather than to her cup. "Does it hurt? The way you do it, I mean. They said you had your own way of doing it."

Lee picked up his cup but watched her. "Who's they?"

"Just people. Around. Girls, mostly, girls you might have helped." Helen wormed her hand from his to fold them both about her raised cup, elbows resting against the edge of the table.

He took a sip. "You done this before?"

"You mean a termination?" she whispered. He nodded. A frown. "With you?"

His face hardened momentarily. "With the other two."

"Oh, no." Her lip twitched and she took a sip to cover it. "It was actually our first time. My first time."

"Didn't think you could get pregnant off the first time?" There was the faintest trace of an acidic smile.

"Well, no. They said—"

"Ah, is this the same they? The girls around?" He put his half empty cup down. "Bit of advice: don't listen. Most of what they're saying sounds . . . ill informed."

She pursed her lips and looked away. "Well."

"Well."

Lee reached into his pocket to take out a folded wad of thin blue plastic and held it out to her. Her eyes flicked about as she let it roll into her palm and clenched her fist around it. Drawing it back to her lap, she inspected the package. Inside the plastic, the substance was doughy with a greasy film. She peeled it open and flinched at the pungent smell. "Cheese?"

He pointed a blunt finger, lifting his cup again. "Nothing you'll ever find in a deli."

Helen thumbed the plastic closed again. "Is this loaded? I thought you didn't use chemicals. There's traces and someone will find out that—"

"You don't eat it," he said flatly. "You put it on your gusset and leave it for ten minutes."

"But." Repulsion was blocked by confusion. "Why?"

"Bourgeonal is a chemical used in perfume for its Lily of the Valley sent. It also acts as a chemoattractant for semen. They'll all swim toward it. In the same way, that they attract foetuses. Strong like that, I've seen them claw themselves out hands first to get at it."

The sounds of street traffic and buzz of the nearby Tesla coils on neighbouring roofs were suddenly deafening before shrinking to freezing white noise. "You can't be serious."

CHEESE

"Just do as I tell you, then come back and drink your tea. It'll help stop your body from going into shock."

Helen jerked her head, lips thin as she hid her hands in her lap. "I can't. This is just . . . "

Lee's eyes brimmed with warnings. "Not changed your mind, have you?"

She gave a shuddered exhale, mouth tipping in a humourless smile. "It's just ridiculous. I mean, it's just one thing. One tiny thing, and you want me to trick it out with cheese."

There was no softening in the lines around his eyes, but they were edged with understanding. "It's all about the one every time, now. You can't fight the numbers." He spoke to his cup with thin humility. "The government isn't going to feed the mouths it wants made. Don't think of it as a potential mouth. It's a number, a one you didn't want yet."

Lee pushed his glasses higher up his nose and looked out of the window, apparently steadfast. Helen sat with the warming cheese in her hand for another few seconds before she stood and went to the toilet by the counter. She spent several minutes inside before she came back with bright hands that smelt of pink soap.

"Now drink your tea," Lee reminded, freshening her cup from the pot and then refilling his own. He noticed her waiting. Feeling. "You won't feel it at this point, not at eleven weeks. And it won't hurt any more than menstrual cramps for a few minutes. Stuff works fast. The tea will help lower your cortisol so your body doesn't panic in response."

Helen drank her tea through her teeth, listening to it froth through the thin gaps. It had cooled and mingled with saliva when it finally reached her throat, bitter without the milk. "What happens next?"

He jerked his arm to shift his sleeve back, checking his watch. The studded face flashed softly in rhythm. "At 2:40 you go back into the toilet. Then you'll wipe out your gusset and pinch through the umbilical cord with your nail. Sometimes the placenta gets dragged out, sometimes not. You'll get a normal period sometime later for the rest."

"And that's it?"

"That's it."

She nodded and clutched her cup. They didn't look at each other for the remaining eight minutes, and she couldn't fathom why he waited with her. There was a rolling discomfort deep in her gut, building but not acutely painful. She examined the rim of her cup so she wouldn't visualize what was happening.

At 2:40, Lee tapped his watch. "You're done." He downed the last dregs of cold tea and stood. "Drinks are included. It's been paid for."

Helen nodded and tucked her hair behind her ears in short, fast strokes, watching his empty seat as his shadow moved across it. When she looked up, he was gone.

She wasn't aware of anything as she walked back to the toilet. Inside the stall, she leant against the locked door and cupped herself through her skirt. There was a wet sort of warmth, but nothing totally alien. An over-soaked tampon, at most.

Sitting on the toilet seat, Helen pulled her underwear down to her knees and bent forward, inspecting her gusset. There, quite clearly, was the foetus. Its blank, egg yolk eyes comprised most of its head, which was gumming at the cheese. Its thin limbs and webbed hands clutched and fleshed at the yellow smear, the peanut body curled. The thread that ran taut from it was bright red and left a thin lash of blood when she put her thumb through it. She could see a down of hair all over it through the slick fluid.

With a ball of rough toilet paper, she dragged the cheese and drying foetus off her gusset, dropping it into the bowl through her thighs. She stood and flushed before she pulled her underwear back up, adjusting her hair blindly as she reiterated that it was just a number she'd subtracted. Then she went back to work.

ABOUT THE AUTHORS

K. TRAP JONES, editor

Trap writes gruesome, funny stories for people who like gruesome, funny stories. As a product of the '80s, he likes his movies bloody and his music heavy. He is the owner of The Evil Cookie Publishing and is the Co-Founder of The Splatter Club. He won the 2010 Royal Palm Literary Award and was nominated for the 2017 Splatterpunk Award. His novels are in the double-digits and he has published over 150+ short stories over the last decade. Trap can be found lurking around metal concerts near Tampa, FL.

BRIAN ASMAN

Brian Asman is the author of the novella *I'm Not Even Supposed to Be Here Today* from Eraserhead Press. His short stories and comics have appeared in numerous anthologies including *Lost Films, Breaking Bizarro*, and *Tales of Horrorgasm*. Brian recently earned an MFA in Creative Writing at UCR-Palm Desert and holds a B.A. in English from the University of Mary Washington. He is a member and former President of the San Diego Chapter of the Horror Writers Association. You can follow him on Instagram @thebrianasman, on Facebook facebook.com/brianasman.14, on Twitter @brian_asman, or visit brianasmanbooks.com. Brian is represented by Jennie Dunham of Dunham Literary, Inc.

ROBERT ESSIG

Robert Essig is the author of over a dozen books including *Stronger Than Hate, Death Obsessed* and *Shallow Graves* (with Jack Bantry). He has published well over 100 short stories and edited several small press anthologies. Robert lives with his family in East Tennessee.

JOHN MCNEE

John McNee is a Scottish horror author known for the books *Prince of Nightmares*, *Grudge Punk* and *Petroleum Precinct*, as well as his extreme horror collection, *John McNee's Doom Cabaret*. He can be found on Facebook, Twitter and YouTube, where he hosts the Vincent Price-themed cooking show *A Recipe for Nightmares*.

KJ MOORE

Dr KJ Moore writes horrible things for horrible people, and has a sordid past leading university students astray. She has two novellas, *Dolls* and *Monster Porn*, that her students used to pass around like dirty notes (irksome, as the class only bought one copy between them). She also has a collection of short stories, *#Horrible*, which no one with a shred of decency should read. Her thesis remains staunchly unpublishable, in part because of the story-critical diptych collage made of torn-up porn mags (how to spend a lovely couple of days with a glue stick and vulva without causing injury). Outside of writing, she enjoys giant robots, imaginary relationships with ineligible people, and a strong cup of Yorkshire tea.

CHANDLER MORRISON

Chandler Morrison is the author of *Along the Path of Torment, Dead Inside, Until the Sun, Hate to Feel*, and *Just to See Hell*. He lives in Los Angeles.

NIKKI NOIR

Nikki Noir writes erotic thrillers, extreme horror, and bizarre plotlines. Books one and two of her *Black Planet* series will be re-released by Blood Bound Books in 2020. Nikki enjoys reviewing all forms of dark fiction, blogging, and teasing her twisted ideas at www.RedRumReviews.com

JOSHUA REX

Joshua Rex is an author of dark and speculative fiction. He lives and works in Providence, Rhode Island.

CM SAUNDERS

Chris Saunders, who writes fiction as C.M. Saunders, is a freelance journalist and editor from south Wales. His work has appeared in almost 100 magazines, ezines and anthologies worldwide, and he has held staff positions at several leading UK magazines ranging from Staff Writer to Associate Editor. His books have been both traditionally and independently published, his latest release being Tethered on Terror Tract Publishing. Find out more at his website: https://cmsaunders.wordpress.com/

AIRIKA SNEVE

Airika Sneve is a writer, musician, and truth seeker from Minnesota. She enjoys envisioning the weirdest scenarios possible and has been doing this in print since 2010. Her greatest inspiration is Edna Luene.

PAUL STANSFIELD

New Jersey born and raised, Paul Stansfield spent decades as a field archaeologist for his day job. Surprisingly, even though he professionally disturbed hundreds of graves, he has yet to suffer a haunting or zombie attack. By night he likes to write horror stories. He's had over 20 stories published by magazines, including such publications as *Bibliophilos, Morbid Curiosity, Cthulhu Sex Magazine, The Literary Hatchet*, and *Horror Bites*. Currently he was stories available in 8 anthologies, including *The Prison Compendium* (EMP Publishing), *Cranial Leakage Vol. 2* (Grinning Skull Press), and *Hidden Menagerie Vol. 1* (Dragon's Roost Press). He's an Affiliate Member of the Horror Writers Association. His personal blog address is: http://paulstansfield.blogspot.com His hobbies include watching professional football and baseball, drinking craft beer, tandem unicycle-spotting, and translating ancient Esperanto books into Silbo Gomero (sometimes all at the same time).

MATTHEW VAUGHN

Matthew Vaughn is the author of *The ADHD Vampire, Mother Fucking Black Skull of Death* and *Hellsworld Hotel*, and *30 Minutes or Less*. With his brother, Edward Vaughn, they edited and compiled *The Classics Never Die! An Anthology of Old School Movie Monsters* for their own press, Red All Over Books. He lives in Shelbyville, Kentucky and is the father of four little children, yet he and his wife are just big kids too. By day he maintains machines and robots, by night he is a writer of Bizarro and Horror fiction. You can keep up with his work at: http://authormatthewvaughn.com/
https://www.facebook.com/AuthorMatthewVaughn
https://twitter.com/mcvaughn138
https://www.instagram.com/m_f_n_black_skull_of_death

MATT WEBER

Matt Weber is owner of Pint Bottle Press, editor of the Double Barrel Horror anthology series, and author of the short story collections, *A Dark & Winding Road, Seven Feet Under* and *Teeth Marks*. Find him online at www.pintbottlepress.com

PATRICK WINTERS

Patrick Winters is a graduate of Illinois College in Jacksonville, IL, where he earned a degree in English Literature and Creative Writing. He has been published in the likes of *Sanitarium Magazine, Deadman's Tome, Trysts of Fate,* and other such titles. A full list of his previous publications may be found at his author's site, if you are so inclined to know:
http://wintersauthor.azurewebsites.net/Publications/ListQ@

Made in the USA
Monee, IL
27 July 2023

40009913R00100